MW01125367

A MERMAID'S HEART

A STEAMY MYTHOLOGY ROMANCE

TAMSIN LEY

A Production of
Twin Leaf Press

ruz watched his friend, Jake, run a finger down the bare arm of an over-tanned blonde and say something that made her giggle. The party boat's deck was loaded with inebriated targets, and apparently Jake was determined to bone every one of them. This vacation was supposed to be a diving expedition, and Jake had told him they'd be snorkeling today, but so far, no one had even dipped a toe in the water.

Cruz caught his friend's eye and signed, "You ready for a swim?"

Jake gave him a wicked grin that told him no and launched into one of his signature jokes.

Sighing, Cruz looked out over the glittering water, imagining the sound of the waves against the hull and the cry of gulls in the distance. Deaf since the age of seven, he vaguely remembered the sounds from TV shows he'd seen. He'd also learned that his voice tended to come off as less than charming, and as a rule remained silent.

The scent of coconut body oil wafted toward him and he returned his attention to the conversation, laughing a little too late—and possibly too loud—at Jake's punch line.

A redhead puckered her brows, her sangria-stained lips forming the words, "What's up with him?"

Knowing Jake was about to pull the deaf card—chicks dug a guy with a deaf friend almost as much as they dug a guy with a puppy—Cruz forced his mouth into a good-natured smile and signed, "Going lobster diving."

Jake lifted his chin in Cruz's direction in acknowledgment and kept talking to the blonde.

Cruz strode to the back of the boat and grabbed a snorkel mask. Diving into the blessedly cool water, he kicked toward a rock overhang in the reef. He'd always loved diving; deafness wasn't an issue underwater. Normally, he preferred full scuba gear, although he did equally well free diving. He had a keen eye for detecting spiny lobsters on the sandy floor and even made enough to pay his rent one summer selling them to a local market.

Within moments, he spotted a blue-green crustacean. He angled in to snatch it by its carapace and was ready to shoot back to the surface when he spotted one of the party girls peeking at him from behind a lacy green sea fan. At least one person had followed his lead and come in for a swim. Her long dark hair billowed around her face, and her bright red lipstick shone vividly even underwater.

Huh. He didn't think any of those women from the boat would actually want to get wet—at least, not with water. His chest was beginning to ache with the need to breathe, but he raised the lobster in greeting and made an eating motion. "Dinner?"

The woman opened her mouth as if to speak, beckoning him toward her with one hand.

She's interested? And she liked to swim, too. Maybe this party boat had been a good idea after all.

Grinning, Cruz pointed to the surface and kicked upward, keeping his eyes on the woman.

A flash of pale skin, black hair, and red... legs? shot toward him in a blur.

Startled, he stopped kicking. A woman with flowing purple hair swept up from behind him, close enough that her naked breasts brushed against his arm. She pulled his face to hers, clamping his lips in a kiss. *This is a bit fast, even for a drunken cruise.* Her hair enveloped him in a purple mist, blocking his vision. The lobster slipped from his fingers. He grabbed her hands, trying to pull them from his cheeks, but damn, the woman had a grip. His lungs burned for oxygen.

The woman not only continued forcing her tongue between his lips but now crushed her breasts and hips against him as if ready to do the nasty right then and there.

What the fuck? Unable to break free, he kicked for the surface for all he was worth, dragging her with him.

A second, distinctly feminine body pressed against his back. The snorkel mask was ripped from his head while two sets of hands slithered greedily over his skin.

He struggled against them, bubbles leaking from his mouth and nose. *How can they hold their breaths so long?*

A hand reached around him and dipped into his trunks, grabbing his shaft.

The air left his lungs in a great rush. *Holy fuck!*

He resisted sucking in that fateful first inhalation of water. This couldn't be real, being mauled to death by beautiful women underwater. His head grew muzzy with the need to breathe. Closing his eyes, he felt like this had to be a bad dream.

A dream. He had to be dreaming. There was no other explanation—unless he was already dead...

He sucked in a draught of water.

And then another.

His eyes opened to the freckled cheeks of the purple-haired woman still enveloping him in a kiss. She rubbed her lithe body against him, her nipples teasing the fine hairs over his pecs.

If this is a dream, I may as well go with it.

Taking hold of the woman's hips, he noted the lack of a bikini bottom. This was the most vivid dream he'd ever had in his life. He swore he could even smell sex rising from her skin, filling the water. He wrapped both hands around the small of her back, pressing his arousal hard into her flesh.

She wriggled in obvious pleasure and broke the kiss to nibble his jawline. While she worked her way down his throat and chest, the woman at his back slithered up over his head to take over the kiss from an upside-down position. Before her halo of hair once again blocked out his surroundings, he imagined he saw a huge, purple tail fin spread out in front of him...

His swim trunks were yanked down his hips.

Much as he loved the ocean, he'd never had a sex dream about it before. *This is awesome.* His entire bloodstream surged with need.

A firm tongue caressed the head of his shaft. His hips jerked involuntarily, and a groan rose from deep in his chest. He didn't know where to put his hands—the woman at his crotch or the woman plunging her tongue into his mouth. He settled for one hand each, knotting his fingers in their hair and kissing back with deft strokes of his tongue. Immediately above his head bobbed his kissing partner's breasts, tipped by nipples as red as maraschino cherries.

Cherries on top, he thought, realizing he was feeling a bit drunk. *Why not?* It was his dream. He could do whatever he desired. He reached up to pull one within reach of his mouth when a third set of hands swept over the breasts. Delicate fingers and golden skin so dark it was closer to brown than gold pinched the nipples, coaxing them into sharp peaks.

Pulling his face from the kiss, he tried to get a better look at his partners, but long-nailed fingers pulled him roughly back into place. Somewhere in the back of his mind, he wondered about the forcefulness of this fantasy. He didn't mind a woman with an appetite but generally liked to do a bit of the steering himself. At the moment he felt like nothing more than a toy.

Three sets of hands and three mouths caressed his skin, his lips, his groin. He couldn't return their touches fast enough, slippery breasts and hard nipples under his palms, a slender neck, silky hair slipping between his fingers. Yet every time he reached for that sweet spot between their legs, they pulled out of reach.

Then one of them grabbed his hips, driving her pelvis against him. The familiar encasing warmth of her nearly made him come. *Holy mother of God, no condom.* Good thing this was a dream. She pumped against him furiously. He reached around and grabbed her ass, only to have her ripped away without warning.

Dark hair filled his vision. Pointed teeth flashed between crimson lips. He blinked, realizing the dark-skinned woman with brilliant gold hair also seemed to have a bright gold tail instead of legs. *What the fuck?* He knew mermaiding was a thing, with costume tails and all, but these women were so damn real.

He attempted to back away, pushing against the crimson-lipped woman's pale shoulders. A small white charm that looked like a turkey wishbone dangled from a cord between her naked breasts. Below her belly button, her flesh brightened to match her mouth. Brightened and coalesced into fins and a tail.

A fish's tail.

Realization exploded inside him like a breath of air after a long dive. He shoved harder, clearing more of his view. The rocks and reef were no longer in sight, nor was the shadow of the party boat at the surface. They'd drifted into a towering kelp forest, the filtered sunlight now hazy and green. Despite his flagging interest, his partners had lost none of their ardor, and continued to claw and thrust and grope, seeming to grow frustrated at his inattention.

Mechanically, he returned their caresses. Gave them what they wanted. If he didn't, he had no idea what might happen. This wasn't a dream, and these were no ordinary women.

He was underwater.

He was breathing.

And he was surrounded by mermaids.

*E*bby peered between the veins of a sea fan toward the orgy of mermaids in the kelp clearing. They passed a deeply tanned human between them, his muscular frame adjusting to their undulations with surprising agility for a land creature. His hands squeezed their breasts or pulled them into coital embraces with what seemed like an uncanny sense about how to prevent the orgy from becoming a violent, competitive frenzy. The current drifting toward Ebby reeked of sex, heightening the uncomfortable urgency low in her belly.

Finish already.

Two years ago, she'd chosen to be female. Not out of any biological urge, but because mermaids were obviously the stronger sex. Mermen like her da were destined to live out slow and miserable death-sentences, bound to the first female they mated with until their mate's unfaithfulness caused their hearts to literally break. Although Ebby was undeniably female now, she refused to be like her mother, killing humans and subjecting mermen to inevitable misery.

With thoughts of her mother's behavior always on her mind, Ebby'd managed to remain a virgin—an unheard-of feat among the females of her kind—and merely watched these orgies from a safe distance, waiting until the unwitting human men were used up and abandoned. Then she swept in and towed them toward shore. Unfortunately, most were killed during the orgy. Those she found who weren't already dead always expired of their wounds during the journey toward land.

But that didn't stop Ebby from trying.

The man she was watching now had held up remarkably well, and she thought she saw signs of the mermaids tiring of him. If she could rescue at least one man from his demise, her abstinence would be worth it.

The mermaids' seductive song rose and fell, Urokotori's crimson claws stroking the twin prongs of the fish harp she wore around her neck. They rubbed their bodies along the human's, pulling at Ebby's instincts as surely as they pulled the male's. She slid one hand over her own pale breast and tweaked the sensitive coral nipple. A shockwave of pleasure rippled into her core.

Pinching her nipple harder, she let her other hand creep to the aching folds of her vulvar slit. Her tail twitched as she rubbed, her blood heating as she watched the man's length slide in and out of a mermaid. On the verge of climax, the orgy drifted close to her hiding spot and red-tailed Urokotori spotted her through the fronds.

"Come on, Ebby." The other mermaid clamped her bony fingers around Ebby's forearm, dragging her hand from her breast and pulling her free of her hiding spot.

Behind her, still half-buried in the sand, Ebby heard her pet mantis shrimp, Kato, shimmy himself deeper beneath the sand. The other mermaids laughed at her for keeping such a useless pet, but Kato had bonded to Ebby of his own accord, not because Ebby compelled him, and Ebby loved everything about him.

"We've all had our turn." Urokotori flung Ebby forward into the man's arms. "He can be your first."

The other two mermaids stopped their songs, pointed teeth gleaming between kiss-swollen lips. Lutana jackknifed and stroked the man's backside with her gleaming golden tail fin. "Humans are so willing to play."

"He has inspiring stamina," Selachii agreed, her amethyst eyes hooded with satiation. Her triggerfish minion wriggled between the grotesquely scarred rip in her freckled tail fin.

The man's gaze met Ebby's, and she was struck by eyes that reminded her of pebbled tidepools. Was that a glint of alarm she saw? He'd been so willing and confident during the orgy, never hinting at fear or exhaustion.

The three mermaids encircled Ebby and pushed the nearly spent man against her. His long, lean thighs brushed her tail, the tip of his erection leaving a trail of fire along her skin. She'd never been this close to an aroused man before.

Urokotori commanded, "Sing, Ebby."

Her attention slid down his muscular chest to his perfectly rippled abs. A line of downy hair traced a path to his bobbing member. Only a few scratches marred his smooth bronze skin where the mermaids had grown careless or rough.

Ebby licked her lips, her nether regions pulsing despite her resolve. How could she escape this? Mermaids could be just as brutal toward their own gender as they were to any man. But she dare not risk getting pregnant. Mermaids were terrible mothers, and Ebby had sworn to never subject a little one to the abandonment and terror she'd endured as a child.

"He's ready," Lutana said. "You don't even need to sing. Just take him and get it over with."

Urokotori shoved between her shoulder blades, driving breasts against the man's hard chest. "Depths, you're boring."

The human's hands found her waist as if by instinct, neither pushing her away nor pulling her closer.

Boring. That was her way out. The only way to escape the attention of a mermaid was to bore them. That, or offer better entertainment elsewhere. She decided a long, slow kiss would be boring enough without inciting their wrath. She'd just have to reign in her own instincts and not take it farther.

To be fair, her only experience kissing had been with Lutana; the golden-tailed mermaid liked women as much as men. Ebby had found some pleasure in her touches, but not enough to keep coming back for more.

The man's hands, however, were different, padded by callouses, and broader than a mermaid's. The sensation of his palms on her skin made her ache with need. How would his thick fingers feel plunging between her folds?

No, Ebby, she chided herself. *A kiss is all you get.*

Placing her hands on the man's shoulders, she pressed her lips against his.

C ruz had attempted to get away from these voracious women only once—and paid the price. A set of bleeding lacerations down his hip still stung from the red-tailed one's claws as she'd pulled him back into an embrace. These females were strong, stronger than humans, and quick. They seemed to be out for more than just sex—they wanted blood.

To his relief, the frenzy seemed to be winding down. But his inner voice was already asking what happened next.

Then the red-tailed mermaid yanked a fourth mermaid from among the weeds surrounding the kelp clearing.

Her apricot tail was flawless and her skin so pale she could have been a ghost. Atop her head, a fiery auburn halo of hair rippled in the current, and her coral nipples beckoned from the perfect peaks of small but luscious breasts. Although she had hips, her legs were fused into a single, supple appendage. Like the other mermaids, her feminine parts were exposed on the front, open to him, inviting his penetration.

But this woman's pulsing folds seemed different. More demure. As if she would've covered herself if she could.

The mermaids seemed to regain their flagging interest upon her introduction, and despite his exhaustion, his manhood surged back to life. Yet where the other mermaids' gazes were feral and hungry, this pale beauty's eyes held... fear? Definitely hesitation. She didn't want to do this. Was being coerced by the others like a freshman girl at a frat party. He found himself wanting to protect her from these other man-eaters.

She was shoved into his arms. The other mermaids were obviously taunting her, threatening her. His hands met her waist, holding her at bay, her skin cool and silky to his touch.

To his surprise, she pressed her lips to his. Not an open, aggressive kiss like the other women. Tight-lipped.

Forced.

Oh, hell no. He was no rapist. These women had already all but forced themselves upon him. He would not be used as an instrument to hurt an innocent.

Her hands came up behind his neck, her breasts teasing the hairs on his chest. Blood surged to his groin, arguing against his resolve, and he dug his fingers harder into her waist, breathing through his nose in an effort to control himself.

He latched onto that sensation, breathing. This wasn't a dream, yet he was somehow breathing underwater. How long would this ability last? What would happen when the mermaids left? He glanced toward the surface, gauging how far it might be and if he could make it before drowning. Damn, he was in real trouble even if the mermaids didn't decide to have him as a post-coital snack.

Seeming to sense his drifting attention, sharp claws raked down his shoulders.

The apricot mermaid kissing him pulled him closer, crushing his hard shaft between them, yet it felt as if she did it to protect him rather than pleasure herself. She didn't buck against him, and her grip on him trembled while the other mermaids continued circling. Although he could feel the pulsing folds of her sex against his hipbone, her mouth remained a rigid line beneath his lips.

Pulling her closer, he eyed the flashes of color from passing fins. His skin flinched at every brush of their clawed fingers. How was he going to get himself out of this, let alone the apricot mermaid?

As he was thinking, claws jerked his head backward. The red mermaid leered at him, hand still tangled in his hair, then turned and hauled him free of the apricot mermaid's grip. Like feeding sea lions, the brightly colored mermaids carried him away, leaving the apricot mermaid gaping in their wake.

*I*t took a moment for Ebby to regain her composure. Then she darted after Urokotori's crimson tail fins, knowing exactly where the other mermaid was heading. While some mermaids cultivated schools of fish or vicious eels as pets, Urokotori kept a giant octopus in a cave not far from here. The mermaids delighted in feeding it, watching its arms and beak rip its meal to pieces—always while that meal was still alive.

"Wait!" Ebby cried as she pushed out of the kelp toward the rock face. Ahead, she spotted one of the octopus's giant red arms retreating back into the cave.

Floating near the entrance, Urokotori smoothed her long black locks away from her face in satisfaction. "That'll keep him."

There was no blood filling the water, yet the human had disappeared from sight. An angry-looking octopus eye filled the cave entrance. Surely the creature couldn't have eaten him that fast? "What did you do?"

Selachii stretched her arms languidly over her head and allowed her triggerfish to shimmy up her side, powerful mouth snapping the water. "Call for me when it's time to play. I'm going to take a beauty rest."

A stream of bubbles escaped Urokotori's lips, and she rolled her eyes. "For all the good *that* will do."

Lutana giggled. Selachii's freckled face darkened and her amethyst hair seemed to stand on end as she turned on her sister.

Ebby drifted backward, sure there was about to be bloodshed.

Urokotori emitted a soft trill and reached for her fish harp. A suckered red arm shot from the cave, tip curling with menace. "Watch it now, sister."

Selachii thrust out her jaw but backed into the kelp forest, disappearing from view.

Smirking, Urokotori turned to Ebby. "Timuri has permission to eat the human if he tries to escape. Don't even think about trying to take him out to play unless I'm here."

Ebby eyed the cave as the octopus resumed its camouflage among the rocks, then nodded. She knew better than to interfere with another mermaid's pet.

With a flick of her tail, Urokotori darted up and over the rock face, headed off to find mischief elsewhere.

Lutana regarded Ebby, her golden eyes not unkind. "How frustrating." Arching her back, she moved closer and ran a tender finger down the top of Ebby's breast and over the nipple. "I can help relieve your tension if you like."

Ebby took the other mermaid's hand to stop further advances. Of all the mermaids, Lutana was the most benign. "I'm fine."

On the ledge below the cave, Kato crept silently over the sand toward her from his hiding spot between some scattered boulders. Coming this close to the octopus's lair was dangerous, and she wished her tiny friend had stayed away. Releasing Lutana's hand, Ebby settled to the ledge and shielded him while he burrowed beneath the sand next to her. She wasn't ready to give up on freeing the man, but she wasn't sure what her next step should be.

"Once, Urokotori kept a man in that cave for over a month." Lutana curled her tail to one side and sat in the sand beside her. "Until she forgot to renew his breath."

"Oh." It was bad enough to use a man, but to imprison him and use him over and over only to let him drown? Despicable.

"Humans are wonderful in how they can love multiple women." Lutana's pretty coral lips pursed into a pout. "But tragically fragile."

Ebby stared at the dark cave opening. "We have to get him out of there."

"I'm not crossing Urokotori." Lutana spread her tail fin and stirred a flurry of debris from the ocean floor. "You saw what she did to Selachii's tail to get that fish harp."

A reflexive shudder passed through Ebby. That fight had been brutal. "Maybe I can offer her something in exchange?"

Ebby didn't spend a lot of time with the other mermaids, so she didn't know what kinds of things they might value, but her mother had liked Da's jewelry. She toyed with the conch-spiral bracelet on her wrist. Da had made it for her just before she entered puberty, telling her it would bring her luck once she chose her gender; he'd always assumed she'd choose to be male.

Her throat felt thick as she remembered the look of disappointment in his eyes when her breasts had emerged.

Lutana watched Ebby stroke the bracelet with avaricious attention. "What are you offering?"

Suddenly uncomfortable, Ebby shrugged. "There's all kinds of stuff buried around that shipwreck."

"Ew." Lutana withdrew her hand. "You expect me to dig in the muck with you? Forget it. And forget him. He's just a pitiful human." She rolled lazily onto her back and pushed off toward the kelp forest. "If you insist on having a male, at least find one of our own kind who can provide you a nest."

As the mermaid's gleaming tail winked out of sight between the fronds, Ebby rose from the sand. There was only one place she could go for advice on this; Uncle Zantu. He'd defeated mermaids before.

"C'mon, Kato." She settled his bony carapace against the crook of her neck and he promptly nestled into her hair, holding tight for the swim.

Giving one final glance at the cave, she darted toward the surface, praying Uncle Zantu could come up with a rescue plan before the poor human's breath-spell expired.

*C*ruz stared at the mottled gray octopus blocking the opening. Its arms had to be longer than he was tall and its bulbous, pulsing head blotted out the dim light entering the cave. Was that the only exit? Why had the mermaids put him in here? Swimming with mermaids definitely hadn't been in the party-boat's brochure.

Keeping one eye on the octopus, he kicked upward, arms outstretched, searching for the ceiling. Hard rock met his fingertips, edges worn smooth by the water. Here and there his fingertips discovered pockets of air trapped between the water and the stone, none more than a few inches in height. How long would his ability to breathe underwater last? At least it hadn't gone away when the mermaids left. Hadn't he read a story about a mermaid's kiss granting water breathing? These mermaids fit the description he recalled, from their beauty to their voracious sexuality.

Using his hands to move along the dark cave ceiling, he reached a wall and followed it downward to the sandy bottom. The cave wasn't small, but it wasn't enormous, either, about the size of a large bedroom. Blinking, he realized he could see, at least a little. Was there a crevice somewhere letting light through? He lifted his gaze and was greeted by a trail of perfect teal-green handprints. Wherever he'd touched the wall now glowed.

Phytoplankton.

He purposefully rubbed his fingertips along the rocks, illuminating the cave's interior with dim green light. Spinning in a slow circle, he gauged his surroundings. The cave walls, though lumpy, had no visible exits except the one the octopus guarded. The sandy floor was littered with empty crustacean shells and a few bones from long-dead fish. He glanced at the creature guarding the entrance.

Someone on the boat must've noticed by now that he'd failed to come up for air. Surely, they'd send divers to look for him. Would they even think to look inside the cave? He needed to get a signal to them. Swallowing, he approached the cave entrance, praying the octopus was as frightened of him as he was of it.

One long gray arm shot out and struck him.

Bubbles burst from his lips and his chest felt like it was on fire as he slammed backward into the cave wall. Green light filled the cave—or was it the stars filling his vision? For a brief moment, he worried the blow had removed his ability to breathe water. Then he shuddered and breath returned to his lungs. *Fuck, that hurt.*

He ran his fingertips over the circular welts rising on his chest and glared at the octopus's pulsing head. The creature eyed him back with hungry intelligence. For all he knew, the thing was saving him for a midnight snack. Did octopuses sleep? Cruz wasn't sure, but he seemed to recall they were night hunters.

Backing up to the wall farthest from the entrance, Cruz kicked away the clutter of shells and settled to the floor. His exertion with the mermaids had tired him out, and he had no idea when they might return. *If* they would return.

He hoped he wasn't on the menu once darkness fell.

*E*bby pulled herself onto a surf-washed boulder and looked up the cliff toward the human dwelling nestled there. Moonlight sparkled off the waves and painted the treetops and rocks silver. She'd never come to her uncle's home at night, and the blackness under the shrubbery surrounding the shoreline made her nervous. Several rectangles of light glowed on the hillside.

Keeping her tail in the lapping waves, she took a deep breath and sang out. The air coming off the shore smelled different in the dark, flowery and verdant yet also hinting at decay.

Her call wavered over the shush of the waves, a request, not a demand. Ebby never sang unless absolutely necessary; forcing other beings to do her will made her feel queasy. Not that she could force Uncle Zantu to do anything; he was immune to mermaid songs since he'd found his true mate.

Soon, a broad-shouldered figure appeared from the path up the hill, accompanied by a smaller figure who darted out ahead. "Ebby!"

Uncle Zantu shouted, "Camilla, stop!"

"It's Ebby, Daddy! I told you!"

Ebby smiled as her cousin splashed headlong into the water toward her. The girl wore a thin gown with a frill at the bottom that molded to her legs and looked vaguely like a tail. Ebby had trouble understanding how a child could have a predetermined sex, but Camilla was definitely female, which was the only reason her father allowed her anywhere near the water. Mermaids generally left female humans alone.

As the tiny figure clambered onto the rock next to her, Ebby patted her head. "Your da is right, you know. I could've been dangerous."

"Aw, I knew it was you. You have a pretty voice."

Uncle Zantu stopped with his toes barely in the froth and put his hands on his hips. "Is everything okay, Ebby?"

He wore a loose shirt, legs poking out below loose, knee-length shorts, but his broad shoulders and narrow waist were still evident, and his piercing silver eyes glittered in the moonlight. His mate, Brianna, seemed to appear out of nowhere, ducking beneath his arm to settle in against his side. Ebby still found it strange to see Uncle Zantu with legs, but she could see why Brianna had fallen in love with him.

"Did I wake you?" Ebby asked.

"We were putting Camilla to bed," Brianna answered, a wry smile twisting her mouth as she looked at her dripping daughter who now held Kato in her lap.

A jealous ache pulled at Ebby. Her own mother had never looked at her that way. She slid back into the surf, keeping only her head above water. "I need your advice, Uncle Zantu."

Uncle Zantu moved to a nearby boulder and sat against it. "It must be pretty important to bring you here in the dark. Go on, then."

Gripping the slippery rock, Ebby told them about the human and the mermaids and the octopus cave. Zantu's fists balled at his side as he listened.

When Ebby finished, Brianna stepped into the water as if ready to go for a swim. "You have to save him!"

"I want to, but I'm not sure how," Ebby said, shifting her gaze to her uncle. "I was thinking of trading Urokotori some of Da's jewelry for him."

"I'd be careful of any deals." Zantu shook his head. "If you make him seem valuable, Urokotori won't let him go."

"What can I do, then?"

Zantu shrugged and rubbed his chin. "Wait until they get bored."

Brianna glowered at her husband. "She can't just skulk around and hope they let him go. What if his breath-spell runs out?"

"Or Urokotori kills him for sport?" Ebby added.

"I have an idea!" Camilla said. "Can you bring in a shark to get rid of the octopus? Like you and Mommy got rid of the mermaids!"

Ebby'd avoided sharks ever since that fateful encounter. "Mermaids can't actually control sharks very well."

Zantu straightened and paced the wet sand. "The idea has merit, though. Why don't you command a school of fish to swim in front of the cave? That might lure the octopus out long enough for you to free the human."

Ebby breathed deeply of the fragrant night air, trying to organize her thoughts. "I don't like to force others to do my bidding just because I'm female. I don't want to be like the rest of the mermaids."

"Believe me, you're not," Zantu and Brianna said at the same time.

"Jinx!" Camilla sang, clapping her hands. "You owe me a coke!"

Her parents laughed and Zantu put his arm around his wife, drawing her close.

Ducking underwater, Ebby rubbed her hands over her face. What would it have been like to grow up with a family like this? *I wish I could talk to Da.* But Da was gone, possibly even dead. Most mermen died of a broken heart after their mates died and children left. Her throat tightened. Surfacing once more, she said, "I don't think

Timuri will leave his post. He's waiting to eat the captive." Kato squeaked and curled into a ball at her words. Then another thought occurred to Ebby. "And what about that poor man? *He* could starve to death before Urokotori grows bored."

"You'd better feed him, then," Zantu said.

What would the human do if Ebby brought him food? She couldn't control the octopus, but she could soothe it enough to slip herself in and out.

Camilla splashed off the rock, jarring Ebby back to attention and sending Kato tumbling into the waves. The little girl bobbed to the surface next to her, little legs kicking furiously. "Kato and I can pick some seaweed for you."

"Thank you, Camilla." Ebby guided the little girl back toward shore. "But I can handle it."

Zantu scooped his daughter from the water. "It's too dark for little nibblers like you to go swimming."

"Come on, Nibbler." Brianna took the girl, propping her on one hip. "It's way past your bedtime. Let's leave Daddy and cousin Ebby to talk."

"But I want to stay."

"Your cousin will come back and visit you soon." Zantu planted a kiss on Camilla's head then another on his wife's upturned mouth before turning back to Ebby. "When it's light out, right, Ebby?"

"Of course." Ebby had been coming to the cove to visit her uncle since before choosing her sex. She'd been sure her uncle would reject her just like Da had, terrified of her new violent nature. But Uncle Zantu hadn't shunned her upon discovering she was a mermaid. He *had* become subtly more cautious when it came to Camilla, however. She could sense him relaxing as his little family disappeared up the dark trail.

Leaning against the submerged boulder, Ebby let the gentle surf push her fins back and forth over the sandy bottom. She could feed the human and keep him alive, but what if his breath-spell expired? The duration of the spell could vary from a few hours to a few weeks, depending on everything from his activity levels to how deep he was beneath the waves. She'd have to remain nearby in case that happened. Then, she'd have to provide the kiss. "I'm scared about renewing his breath-spell."

"Why?" Still fully clothed, Zantu moved deeper into the water, allowing the wavelets to slosh over his shoulders.

He said he didn't miss having a tail, but he still loved the water as if it was home.

"What if I... lose control?" Recalling the sight of him pleasuring the other mermaids sent a tingle straight to her core. She thought back to how the human's touch had felt on her waist. The alluring heat of his erection against her hip.

"I don't think you have to be cruel or out of control just because you have breasts." Zantu gazed up at the moon. "The only thing we really have any control over is ourselves. I believe if you want to overcome your mermaid 'nature,' you can."

"But how can anyone defeat nature? Isn't that by definition undefeatable?"

Zantu lowered his chin into the water, silver eyes glinting in the moonlight as he turned his gaze toward her. Then he slowly rose, letting the water mold his thin clothing against his very masculine form. He was her uncle, but he was still a gorgeous man, impossible not to notice.

Flushing slightly, Ebby pointedly turned her gaze skyward.

He made a small, satisfied noise and sloshed back to shore. "You've been coming to see me for over two years now and never once has your 'nature' caused you to do anything inappropriate." Pausing on the bank, he looked over his shoulder at her. "I think most mermaids use 'nature' as an excuse to do whatever they want and not feel bad about their actions later. You're not like that. I have confidence in you." He resumed trekking up the path inland, speaking loud enough for her to still hear him over the waves. "Now, go do what you need to do to save that human. And yourself."

Ebby wanted to ask what he meant by that, but he was already gone.

5

*C*ruz felt the bite of the seatbelt against his scrawny chest. The smothering punch of the airbags trapping him in place. The roar of tearing metal and breaking glass. The scream of his mother...

And jolted awake.

The familiar panic that had haunted his dreams since he was seven was replaced by disorientation of a different kind. His arms and legs churned, unable to find solid ground in the darkness. *Where the hell am I?* Heart racing, everything came back to him. The cave. The orgy. The mermaids... Had any of that really happened?

He took a cool breath of—water. Yep. He was still underwater. The mermaids must be real. Settling his

A MERMAID'S HEART

bare feet back against the sandy floor, he located the patch of light at the cave entrance to orient himself, then floated upward, touching the ceiling. The phytoplankton ignited.

Hoping the octopus might have abandoned its station, he edged forward.

A knobby head and eight, suckered arms lurked at the opening, mottled skin blending against the stone. The thing's gills sucked in and out rhythmically as one bulbous eye swiveled in his direction.

This time Cruz halted shy of getting the stuffing knocked out of him. If he got out of this alive, his nightmares about the accident were going to have company.

A shadow blocked the light. Once. Twice. Cruz swallowed, wondering what could possibly happen next. He scoured the floor for a weapon. The scattered shells and bits of bone were too small to be useful.

The octopus curled in on itself, color shifting from mottled gray to deep red. Cruz tensed, sure an attack was coming. Instead of pouncing, the creature edged aside and the finned silhouette of a mermaid entered.

37

It felt as if the pressure of the water intensified, and Cruz forced himself to take a deep breath, acutely feeling his nakedness. What would be expected of him now?

The cave walls illuminated all at once, bathing everything in monochromatic green light. The apricot-tailed mermaid floated there holding a large, scalloped clamshell.

She moved forward, eyes wide as she studied him. He took the opportunity to examine her, too, now that he was no longer distracted by the need to fend off a violent orgy. Pert breasts topped by darker nipples accentuated her slender figure. She wore no clothing but did have a bracelet around one wrist and what looked like a bone needle dangling from one of her earlobes. Her delicate, fluttering tail fins reminded him of a woman wearing an evening gown in the wind. His gaze drifted lower, to where her sex should be, and saw no more than a discreet slit in her scaleless, apricot tail.

As if embarrassed by his attention, she thrust the clam toward him.

He'd never been a fan of raw shellfish, but refusing a gift might be interpreted as an insult. If he wanted to get out of here, he needed to play nice. He kicked toward her, hand extended.

She drew back, releasing the shell before he had a firm grip. It drifted to the floor, its two halves separating. An assortment of seaweed spilled out, drifting slowly to the sandy floor.

He blinked at it. Why had she brought him a shell full of seaweed?

She looked from the spilled contents to him and back. Features pinched, she sank to the cave floor and began gathering the bits together.

Okay, these were valuable for some reason. Moving slowly, he helped pick up the leaves, placing them back into the half-shell. She once again offered the shell to him, this time open like a platter.

He shook his head and signed, "What am I supposed to do with it?" He was used to signing whether people understood him or not. Most of the time his motions helped them get a sense of what he meant.

An uncertain smile lifted one corner of her lips. From between her fiery auburn tresses, two long antennae emerged, followed by the alien-looking face of a mantis shrimp. The antennae waggled, and Cruz could swear the creature was looking straight at him. The mermaid plucked out a green bit and placed it in her mouth, chewing and swallowing, then offered him the shell again.

Was he supposed to eat it? *Can't be any worse than raw clam.* Choosing a bit that looked a little less alien than the others, he put it into his mouth and chewed. He wasn't usually much of a salad eater, but the seaweed tasted okay—crunchy and salty, although weirdly rubbery.

The mermaid nodded in satisfaction and once more backed toward the exit.

He grabbed her wrist with his other hand and signed, "Stay. Please."

The mermaid stiffened, eyes going wide. She opened her mouth, the lines of her throat rippling with sound he couldn't hear. He could, however, feel a slight vibration through his hold on her wrist. Something about it made his insides flutter. Still, he held tight. She was his only hope to get past the octopus.

The green light filling the cave fluttered and rippled in response to her song. It reminded him of the first time

Jake had dragged him to a rock concert and he'd discovered he could feel the beat even if he couldn't hear it. He'd been a fan of rock concerts ever since. She shut her mouth and stared at where he still held her wrist, then back to his face.

Cruz once again gestured to himself and then the door. "Can I go?"

The mermaid's delicate eyebrows drew together. Tilting her head, the mermaid moved her lips again.

He tapped a finger to his ear then lips, signing, "I'm deaf."

She blinked, gaze following his movement. Hopeful, he pointed at the door again.

Her features transformed into regret and she shook her head. She waggled her fingers in the direction of the octopus, then pointed to him and made a grabbing motion.

Well, that was obvious. The octopus would stop him if he tried to leave. But she seemed to have some control over the animal, so why couldn't she tell it to let him go? He made the sign for octopus and then pointed at her and made the sign for swim. "Can't you get me past?"

She smiled, sharp teeth gleaming between her lips. His insides leapt in alarm, but the smile was without malice. She pointed to herself then the cave door, nodding. Then pointed at him and once again shook her head no.

So, she could pass, but he couldn't.

They seemed to be doing fairly well at the sign language thing, so he asked, "Why not?"

All she did was shake her head again. He wondered if the reason had anything to do with the other mermaids. Regardless, she couldn't or wouldn't help him leave, at least not yet. She tugged her wrist free of his grasp and backed away.

He'd heard what one should do if taken hostage was to make yourself human, but he wasn't sure if that would work when one had been captured by mythical creatures. *Hot mythical creatures.* Jake would advise him to get her name and number. What if he treated her like a woman instead of a jail-keeper?

Pointing to his chest, he followed it by his nickname in sign language, cupping his hands and bumping them forward like a boat. Calling himself Cruise was a lot easier than hand spelling Cruz to people, and he often got a laugh out of it.

She froze, watching his movement.

He repeated the motion a couple of times, then pointed at her. "Your name?"

Comprehension dawned on her features. She seemed to think a moment, then moved her hands like a falling tide. Cute. He liked that. Ebbing tide. One name was as good as another right now. He repeated the motion and smiled. "Good to meet you, Ebby."

He couldn't tell in the pale light, but it seemed like she flushed. His insides churned. He needed to convince her to get him out of here before any of her friends showed up. Those mermaids had been quick to heat up. Perhaps physical contact would help convince her to set him free.

Edging closer, he licked his lips, brushing her arm with his fingertips.

The mermaid's eyes widened. She spun and fled the cave, leaving nothing but churned up sand in her wake.

6

*E*bby raced past Timuri and into the kelp forest as fast as her fins would carry her. Cruz had been immune to her song, but she was apparently not immune to her own desire. The way he'd licked his lips and moved forward had sent immediate heat flooding from her nipples to her belly... and lower.

On top of that, he was quite charming, speaking to her with his hands. Mermaid magic gave her accelerated understanding of all languages, but not instantaneous. She'd need a few more interactions to become fluent in this new form of speech and might actually enjoy getting to know this human.

She shook her head and swam faster, weaving between the swaying kelp fronds as if being chased by a killer whale. Remaining near him would be dangerous for both of them.

After a few laps across the current, she paused, blood pumping in her ears. Kato edged tentatively out of her hair and made a little ticking noise, stroking her cheek gently with an antenna. "Thanks, Kato. I'm okay."

What was it about this human that sent her into a panic when he touched her? She'd never been this affected by any of the other humans she'd tried to save. He moved with a grace she'd never seen before, more sensual. She remembered the way he'd pleasured the other mermaids and her insides tightened. For the first time, she truly understood why the other mermaids used men like they did. It was difficult to think of anything but relief when her core was crying to be filled.

She ran a flattened palm down her belly as if that act of will could banish the physical sensations threatening to consume her. If she didn't get control of herself, the human would die. Maybe not by her hand, but by any other number of things that could happen. Humans were not meant for the sea.

"If only we could get rid of Timuri," she said absently.

Kato reached out a claw and tugged on her earring, a gift from Lutana back when Ebby'd first introduced herself to the other mermaids. The jewelry was actually a needle-like dart infused with the deadly toxin of a sea snake. "Every mermaid needs an exit strategy," Lutana had said.

But killing another mermaid's pet was taboo and would unite the others against her, putting a death sentence on Ebby's head. She pulled the earring free of Kato's grasp. "You know we can't."

The mantis shrimp sighed in disappointment and slumped against her shoulder, curling his tail behind her shoulder blade.

A school of señorita fish flashed by, drawing her attention. She followed the sharply choreographed movement, listening to them chirp at each other and thinking of Uncle Zantu's suggestion. Just because she directed fish past the cave didn't mean Timuri would catch any, right? The school might distract him from his duty long enough for her to extract the man, Cruz. "You think they can out-swim Timuri?"

Kato purred and scurried backward into her hair, readying himself for a swim.

Ebby sighed and nodded, out of ideas. Taking a loop around a rock spotted with palm-shaped corals, she drove the fish toward the cave.

At the edge of the kelp forest, the fish hesitated, unwilling to leave cover. On the other side of the swaying stalks, Timuri waited just inside the cave opening, his skin blending perfectly with the surrounding rock. Sea fans and coral spotted the cliff outside, but other sea life knew to stay far away from the giant octopus's grasp. Swallowing, she realized she was going to have to command these fish to move in that direction. *It's an emergency*, she told herself. But using her magic on these poor creatures was unfair.

A flash of crimson caught the corner of her eye and she pulled back into the forest just in time to see Urokotori somersault playfully over the edge of the cliff.

The crimson-tailed mermaid pirouetted at the entrance, shook out her hair, and let forth a song of command. Urokotori had no qualms about using her magic on other beings.

The giant octopus cleared the entrance, arms coiling and beak clacking. Kato withdrew further into Ebby's hair.

Urokotori continued singing, the notes shifting from command to seduction.

After a few moments, Cruz's tanned face appeared. Unmoving, he watched Urokotori undulate to her own song, her red fins flared in a full display of desire. Was he truly immune? The song was powerfully hypnotic. Almost strong enough to draw Ebby into its grip. She gripped a slippery kelp trunk in one hand and resisted.

The human remained in the entrance, regarding the dark-haired mermaid. Ebby still didn't understand how, but it was very obvious he was not compelled.

Urokotori's spine stiffened as she seemed to sense something wrong. Ebby's gut clenched. If the mermaid found out Cruz was immune to her, she'd likely kill him outright.

Darting forward, Ebby circled Urokotori, hoping to distract her. "I've been waiting for you."

The other mermaid's black eyebrows drew together and her red lips curled into a sneer. "You're still here? Go away. You had your chance."

"You said you'd share. That I should come back to play." Ebby paused, blocking the older mermaid's view of the cave entrance. Cruz wouldn't be able to swim fast enough to escape, but she could perhaps keep Urokotori from verifying he'd been unaffected by her song. Looking over her shoulder at the cave, she let out a trembling note of seduction and signaled for him to come out. She'd never sung that song before and a part of her rebelled its use now. *He's immune. He won't be affected*, she reminded herself.

His gaze flickered warily between her and Urokotori before he edged forward into the current.

Urokotori elbowed Ebby aside, shoving her hard against one of the nearby spiked coral. The abrasive edge cut into Ebby's hand and the hint of blood filled the water. *Great.* Now she'd be drawing every nearby predator to this location.

Timuri's arms flexed and his beak clacked.

Ebby backed away. "When did you last feed your pet?"

Urokotori shrugged and gestured to Cruz, who had drifted several meters away. "My pet will have a meal soon enough."

The octopus must've taken that as an invitation. One arm flashed out, grabbing Cruz around the ankle.

Instinctively, Ebby let out a sharp trill of command. To her surprise, the creature halted its attack. Taking control of another mermaid's pet was not only difficult but also highly taboo.

"How dare you!" Urokotori seemed to swell in size, her hair fanning out like a nest of sea snakes.

Ebby held her ground. "If you're going to kill the human, be merciful and do it quickly. He's at least earned that." She had no desire to see Cruz killed, but a quick death would be better than being eaten alive.

Urokotori sneered, her teeth sharper than Ebby remembered. "Why, Ebby, I think you like him. Have you been playing with my toys without me?"

Ebby licked her lips, heart beating painfully against her ribcage. Uncle Zantu'd warned her not to make Urokotori believe the man had value. Yet if Cruz had no value, he'd be octopus food. What other choice did she have? She pulled Da's bracelet from her wrist. "Let him live and I'll give you this."

Urokotori reached for the intricately carved shell.

Ebby yanked it out of reach. "Promise me."

The other mermaid's eyes narrowed to slits. Her crimson lips spread wide. "You may buy him one more day with that bauble. Tomorrow he belongs to Timuri. Unless you can bring me another gift?"

"Perhaps," Ebby answered, handing over the jewelry and reigning in her smile. If she'd known freeing the man would be this easy, she would've made this trade long ago, despite the hollow feeling in her stomach about losing her da's trinket. But Da would approve. Cruz would be safe on land by tomorrow. She waved a hand as if the bracelet was indeed no more than a bauble. "I'll bring you more if he pleases me."

Urokotori laughed, shoving the bracelet onto her wrist and crossing her arms. She eyed Cruz lasciviously. "Well, he did have me coming back for another round. I suppose he's worthy of a first time for you. Timuri, put him back."

Ebby stiffened. "You said he's mine."

Urokotori arched a brow. "I said he could live one more day. I didn't say where."

"That wasn't what I traded—"

Once again, the crimson mermaid seemed to swell, her obviously superior power radiating in waves that made the current seem to run in reverse. "That is exactly what you traded for. If you don't like it, don't come back."

All Ebby could do was watch helplessly as the octopus settled in to guard the entrance once again.

With Kato's clawed feet irritating the back of her neck, Ebby floated outside the cave, too flustered and angry to enter. Urokotori had tricked her out of her bracelet.

"You can go on in, darling," the mermaid sang. "There's not much room inside for acrobatics, but I'm sure you can manage."

As the red-tailed mermaid rounded up a nearby school of Garibaldi fish, Ebby fantasized about using her mother's fish harp to call every nearby predator to tear the other mermaid and her pet to shreds. Not that she'd ever learned to play the instrument; it lay securely inside Da's treasure chest along with the stash of jewelry he'd hoarded in the hope of impressing his mate.

At least Urokotori fed her pet, clapping gleefully as the octopus grabbed the orange fish from the current with multiple arms and snapped them in two with its beak.

Ebby shuddered. Timuri, having been fed, would be impossible to lure away. And Urokotori would probably demand another payment at sunup. Until Ebby came up with another plan, she'd have to offer a second trade.

Turning, she sped into the kelp forest. The sunlight glancing off the surface overhead told her night would fall soon. She meandered around the towering kelp, looping back on herself a few times to be sure she wasn't being followed. Mermaids didn't build or keep nests, but she'd tried to maintain Da's, along with his jewelry box. In the vanishing light, she brushed aside sea fans and wriggled sideways between dense kelp stalks into the clearing.

Kato immediately clambered free of her hair and went to work snipping back the overgrown sea sponges that had once served as her father's bed. A gray layer of sediment covered everything, from the tall mirror Da had propped upright with a pile of stones to the waterlogged barrels they'd used as chairs. She'd need to come back here soon and do some maintenance or there wouldn't be any nest left.

Tugging the small jewelry chest free from the sand that had accumulated around it, she set it on the flat stone she and Da had used as a table and pried up the brass latch. The lid, however, refused to open. The light was fading quickly, but she examined the hinges. They seemed corroded, and barnacles had crusted over one corner.

Lying back on the sponges, Ebby stared up at the violet light illuminating the water above. "How am I going to select something to trade if I couldn't even open the box?"

Kato swept sand off the tabletop with short, fast brushes of his tail, seemingly content to have something to do.

Ebby sighed. Would Cruz know how to get the chest open? She didn't really want to take the entire chest with her; if Urokotori saw how much she had, she'd up her price for sure. Not to mention Mother's fish harp was inside. But how else was she going to come up with something to buy his freedom?

Knowing Urokotori might decide their deal broke at dawn, she tucked the jewelry box beneath one arm. "Kato, you coming?"

The mantis shrimp sighed, giving a last flourish of his tail that sent a cloud of sand drifting from the table before joining her. Ebby hurried back to the cave, dodging a school of night-feeding damselfish and humming a sonic warning to ward off any large predators who might be lurking nearby.

When she arrived at the cave entrance, full darkness enveloped the sea floor. Where was Urokotori? A quick, sonic query revealed only open water. A painful knot formed inside Ebby's stomach. The other mermaid had only promised he'd live another day, not that she wouldn't use him. Was she inside the cave with Cruz right now?

Ignoring Timuri's curious gaze, Ebby pushed inside, singing the phytoplankton on the wall to life. To her relief, Cruz was both alive and alone.

Then she realized what that meant.

She was alone with a lithe, naked man.

Uncle Zantu's words of confidence came back to her. *I have confidence in you.* She could do this.

7

*W*orking in almost complete darkness, Cruz rubbed the broad edge of the clamshell bowl on the rock wall, pausing now and again to test the shell's sharpness. He hoped it might serve as a weapon of sorts. The way that red-tailed mermaid had smiled at him with those wickedly pointed teeth made him believe she had more than another orgy in mind. If he couldn't seduce his way out of this situation, he'd fight his way past the octopus and escape. However, if Ebby showed back up...

He wasn't entirely sure what to think of the apricot-tailed mermaid. His first instinct had been to protect her. Well, not really the first instinct. The memory of her lips against his caused a tightening low in his stomach. He shook it away.

She seemed to be protecting him. She'd fed him. Given him her name. Even done something to stop red-tail from... whatever she'd planned.

He halted his sharpening, staring at the glittering phytoplankton that had scraped free of the wall and now floated like tiny teal diamonds around him. He hardly knew Ebby, but the gushy sensation she created in his belly was unlike anything he'd experienced before. He needed to stay rational if he wanted to get out of here alive.

The cave filled with sudden light, and he twisted toward the entrance, clutching his shell in preparation for combat. Ebby floated in the doorway, a small box under one arm. Heart racing, he wasn't sure what to do. Part of him wanted to hide the weapon from her in embarrassment.

She didn't seem to notice his warring emotions, setting the box on the cave floor. The mantis shrimp hiding in her hair scurried down her arm and sat atop the box like a miniature guard dog. A smile twitched the corner of Cruz's mouth, despite his uncertainty. Why didn't it surprise him that Ebby had a shrimp for a pet?

She floated uncertainly in the doorway. Her pale arms were bare of the heavy bracelet. What had she traded it for? Obviously not his freedom or the octopus wouldn't have stuffed him back in here. Did he belong to Ebby now? For long moments, they exchanged silent stares. *Apparently, the first move is up to me.* But what that move was, he didn't know. Certainly not this silly shell weapon he was holding. He set the shell on the sand behind him.

When he looked back up, she pointed to the shell, then signed, "More?"

A flush rose up his neck, and he had to avoid glancing to the corner where he'd discarded the seaweed. She thought he was hiding the shell because he'd eaten it all. He shook his head. "What happened out there with Red-tail?"

She watched his hands carefully, a cute little pucker appearing between her eyebrows. "Food?"

Ah, hell. For a moment, she'd made him forget she didn't understand sign language. 'Food' and 'more' were just baby words even toddlers could master.

He sighed. Circling his wrist with his other hand to indicate "bracelet," he pointed to her now bare wrist.

"You traded," he signed. "Why?"

Her face radiated uncertainty, then she nodded and repeated the wrist-circling motion. "My bracelet."

Most people didn't try to sign, expecting him to read lips. She was making attempts to talk to him with her hands. Warmth spread through his chest. He made the sign for trade again then pointed at himself. "Traded for me?"

She nodded and signed, "Traded my bracelet for you."

Damn, putting sentences together already. She was a fast learner. He pointed at the dark opening. "Can I go?"

Her eyes were sad as she shook her head. "I traded my bracelet," she signed, adding, "One day."

That gushy feeling rose inside him again. She obviously wanted more dialogue than simple pointing, which was better interaction than he'd had with a woman in a long time. He tamped down on his excitement. *Focus on the goal. Escape.*

The other mermaid was obviously the leader, but Ebby'd bought him a single day of reprieve from whatever was to be his fate. "What happens after one day?"

Ebby shook her head, eyes suddenly growing fierce. She pointed to the box she'd set on the floor earlier. "Open."

The box was covered in barnacles and the wood was swollen, but he now recognized it for what it was: a jewelry box. He reached for it.

The shrimp guarding the box took an aggressive stance, tail raised and pointed legs stiff. Cruz knew mantis shrimp could pack a wallop if threatened, delivering a blow that rivaled a small caliber bullet in force. He'd never heard of one attacking a human, but his world had been turned upside down by the impossible already today. He wasn't about to risk a misunderstanding. He paused and turned back to Ebby. "You want me to open it?"

She nodded and shooed the shrimp away. It scuttled to the back wall and quickly buried itself in the sand.

Cautiously, he knelt on the sandy bottom next to the small chest, watching Ebby from the corner of his eye. She wrung her hands, brow furrowed. The lid refused to budge. Looking up at her, he signed, "It's locked."

She bit her bottom lip. "You can't open it?"

He frowned. How did she suddenly know so many words? He gave her a hard look. It was one thing to put a few words together, but her vocabulary was growing by leaps and bounds. "Do you know sign language?"

She shrugged and pointed at him. "I learn fast."

He blinked, unsure he understood correctly. "You learned it from me? But how? We've hardly spoken."

She shrugged one shoulder. "Mermaid magic."

His eyes tracked the hand she fluttered below her waist to say mermaid and when he looked back at her face, she was flushed. *Damn*, she was intriguing. And the topic of magic wasn't even what had him most intrigued. He felt like he was on a first date, having a conversation over dinner. He had so many questions for her, he didn't know where to begin.

"Please, can you open it?" she asked again.

Feeling an unexplainable urge to please her, he examined the latch. Among his many jobs, he'd spent a brief time as a locksmith. But this wasn't a matter of popping a lock. Barnacles had glued the seam together along two edges and the hinges were corroded beyond use. Turning it on its side, he rubbed his fingers over the seam. "I could try to break it."

The sadness on her face made him reconsider. This chest obviously meant something to her. He glanced around the cave floor and his gaze lit on the big clam shell he'd been sharpening. It might be strong enough to pry open the lid with minimal damage.

He picked it up and dug it into the seam at one corner. The waterlogged wood indented, but when he applied pressure, the shell broke, leaving a nick in his honed edge. *Ah, hell.* So much for his weapon.

Using another section of the shell, he chipped off the barnacles and pried again, more carefully this time. After a few minutes, he managed to widen a crack large enough for his fingers, and from there, he forced the hinges to grate open.

Ebby beamed at him, a smile brighter than the gleaming contents of the box. The gushy feeling flooded from Cruz's stomach to his head. He grinned back before realizing what he was doing. *This has to be Stockholm Syndrome.* The funny thing was, at this moment, he didn't care.

Trying to get hold of himself, he focused down at the treasure. Loose shells, pearls, and bits of shiny glass were interspersed with man-made items. A teardrop diamond earring. A filigreed silver bracelet. A thick gold chain. "What is all this for?"

Her smile wavered. "I trade for you."

He had no idea what Ebby's motives were, but he was grateful. There had to be thousands and thousands of dollars' worth of gold and jewels in here. In one corner of the box rested a silk-wrapped bundle not much larger than a cell phone. He picked it up and opened it to reveal a strange white shell with long, thin prongs tipped in gold. A tiara? He placed it on his head and gave her a playful wink, trying to make her smile. "Where did you get this?"

Her face looked stricken.

He sobered, gently folding the silk back around it. "Sorry. I didn't mean to be disrespectful."

She made an attempt at smiling and signed awkwardly, "My mother's."

Ah, hell. She was giving up family jewelry for him? Now he felt really guilty.

"I also find much on shipwrecks." She took the tiara from his hands and unwrapped it once more. Offering him the silk, she gestured toward his hips, her face pinkening. "Humans like to cover?"

He accepted the cloth gratefully, tying it around his hips like a kilt.

"Hand language is new to me," she signed. "Do many humans speak it?"

The comfort that had been developing between them crumbled. Why did it always come back to his disability? "Sign language is for deaf people."

"Deaf?" She repeated his motion, gaze curious. "This means you cannot hear?"

He nodded, steeling his spine. He received one of two reactions from women when they realized he was deaf: pity or disdain.

But Ebby seemed... excited. "You're very lucky to be deaf."

He laughed. *Lucky?* Why on Earth would she consider him lucky? "I don't think lucky is the word you mean."

Her lashes fluttered as she seemed to consider. "Favored?"

He shook his head. "Not that, either."

She pursed her mouth. "I try to say you have advantage."

Now it was his turn to purse his mouth. She did indeed mean lucky. "Why do you say I have an advantage?"

"You cannot be controlled by mermaid song." She glanced over her shoulder toward the dark cave exit. "But you must pretend to be if... I do not know how to say name... Red-tail? sings."

So, the mermaid myths were true. They could control a man by singing. What could they possibly have wanted him to do that he hadn't already done? Didn't mermaids want to drown sailors or something like that? "What does she want?"

Her fists knotted at her sides. "Songs force humans to play."

He widened his eyes. "Play?" All at once, he realized what she meant; the first orgy had been merely the beginning. "You mean sex?"

Cheeks flushed, she turned slightly toward the door. "Much, yes. But also, other sensation."

Her blush warmed his own blood. "Other sensation. What does that mean?"

She gestured to the octopus. "Swim chase. Torture harm. All is entertainment."

His veins went from hot to cold in an instant. After he'd been stuffed back into the cave, a school of fish had come near the entrance, pursued by the red-tailed mermaid. The octopus had snatched them up, churning up blood and debris while the red-tailed mermaid laughed and clapped at the carnage. "Red-tail wants to feed me to the octopus?"

Ebby slumped and nodded. "Probably."

He'd suspected as much, but the confirmation made his heart race. He had to get out of here. The sooner the better.

8

*E*bby watched the expressions drifting across Cruz's face with fascination. Learning a language was as much about connecting body language to words as it was about putting words together, and she found Cruz's rugged features mesmerizing. The firm line of his jaw had grown darker with a line of stubble, and his short dark hair had a tiny bit of curl to it. Hazel eyes seemed to speak to her even when his hands were still, and his mouth...

Heat rose in her cheeks, and she dropped her gaze. Their brief kiss seemed branded on her lips, making her yearn for another. Thank Neptune she'd salvaged that silk so he could at least cover his lower half. Just thinking about what lay beneath the thin fabric gave her flutters low in her belly.

His hand moved toward her and she backed away. "You must not touch me."

He dropped his arm and sifted his fingers through the contents of the treasure box instead. After a moment, he signed, "Why are you helping me?"

She licked her lips. The question was more complex than he could imagine. How easy it would be to give in to her nature and take him. Use him up. But another part of her nature held onto the memory of her da and her resolve to never be like either of her parents. She rubbed her arm, feeling naked without the bracelet she'd used as a reminder of her vow. "I am not like other mermaids."

He smiled, teeth dazzling in the cave's bioluminescent glow. "I know."

The affirmation made her heart swell and her throat tighten. A happy note rose within her, causing the phytoplankton lights to flicker in joyful response.

Cruz glanced around, mouth slightly parted as he watched the ripples race along the walls. He seemed enthralled by the display, so she strengthened her notes and directed the tiny creatures to wink on and off in firework bursts and rolling waves and nautilus swirls.

When she'd finished, Cruz turned back to her, eyes alight. "You did that?"

She nodded.

One side of his mouth quirked up in a sly smile. "Much better than red-tail's entertainment."

Heat once again filled her face. *Depths*, how could he continually make her feel like this? She turned away and studied the wall as if it was the most interesting thing in the world. A noise inside the cave made her stiffen, and she spun, sure Urokotori had snuck up on her.

Only Cruz was here. He signed, "How am I breathing underwater?"

"Mermaid magic." She moved to the cave doorway and peered outside. No one. Turning back, she asked, "Did you hear a noise?"

Cruz's face reddened, and he pointed to himself, opening his mouth. "Hey." Then he signed, "I wanted to get your attention, and you said not to touch you."

Her jaw dropped. Had he lied to her? Why? "You said you're deaf!"

He shook his head. "Deaf means I can't hear. I can speak, just not well."

She moved closer. "How?"

His face hardened, making him difficult to read, but the lines of his throat moved in a swallow; whatever he had to tell her must be painful. "I lost my hearing when I was seven. Before that, I used my voice."

"Lost? Can you find it again?"

He cracked into a smile, but his sadness still made her heart ache. "No. Broken might be a better word. Destroyed. I will never hear again." His gestures were sharp. He pushed his shoulders back as if shaking off that line of questioning. "So, this spell makes me... what? A merman, now?"

She laughed and shook her head. "You won't grow a tail. That magic is beyond mermaids."

"But I'll always be able to breathe underwater?"

Oh. That's what he was asking. She pressed her lips together and shook her head. "The magic must be renewed."

He blanched. "What happens if it expires?"

"I'll get you out of here before that happens." She looked at the treasure chest, wondering how much she would have to give Urokotori to make that happen.

The items inside all had sentimental value, but none were as precious to her as the bracelet she'd already relinquished. None except the fish harp. That was the one item she could never let Urokotori lay hands on. Bending, she pulled the instrument from the chest, stomach churning with memories.

Da never knew she'd gone looking for it after her mother's death. Her mother had lured Da and countless other mermen into compliance with its melodies. Da always joked that the magic in the harp could convince a sea turtle to leave its shell. The delicate instrument was made from a rare sea sponge found in the deepest parts of the ocean. Although one tine had been broken when Ebby located it at the bottom of the Wild Deeps, the nine, remaining gold-tipped tines were exponentially more powerful than Urokotori's smaller harp.

Ebby'd never used a harp. She didn't dare. It embodied everything she despised about mermaids.

"The other mermaids must never lay hands on this harp."

"It's a harp! How do you play it? Like a juice harp?"

"No. This is a fish harp." She touched the tines, careful not to evoke a note. "It's very rare, even among mermaids. It increases the power of our song a hundredfold. The more tines, the more powerful. Mermaids don't need to be any stronger than we already are."

Looking around the cave, Ebby went to the corner where Kato had buried himself and dug a hole next to him. The shrimp's eyes were all that showed above the surface, following her every move. Settling the harp carefully in the depression, she pushed the sand back over the top. "Guard this with your life, Kato."

The shrimp would do just that, although if one of the mermaids discovered it was here, they wouldn't hesitate to kill him, despite his position as Ebby's pet. Kato bobbed his eye stalks in silent acknowledgment, cautious with the octopus so nearby.

Ebby returned to the chest and pulled out a few other pieces. Everything looked rather dull under the blue-green light. Her heart sank as she contemplated which items Urokotori might prefer.

She held up a thin chain which she remembered being rose-gold in the sunlight. Now it looked like nothing more than a fisherman's string.

Strong fingers brushed hers as Cruz caressed the length of the chain. Her stomach jumped into her throat and she released the chain.

With a deft twist, he had the clasp undone and held it toward her. "May I?"

The necklace seemed to have regained some of its brilliance in his hands and she found herself nodding.

He reached around her, within a hairsbreadth of touching her, and latched the chain. His shoulder hovered close enough to kiss if she bent her head. She resisted, her insides fluttering. This close, his refreshing herbal scent permeated the water and made her skin tingle with desire. How the depths was she going to carry him to the surface once she freed him if she couldn't even be near him without losing her mind?

Settling the thin strand so it barely dipped into the hollow between her breasts, he pulled back, his gaze caressing the path of the chain along her collarbone. Slowly, he signed, "Beautiful."

If she'd been flustered before, now she felt completely unstrung. Heat filled not only her face, but her entire body. She couldn't look away. Nothing in this ocean could be half as fascinating as this human. Backing away, unsure of what she was asking, she signed, "Please don't."

"Did I touch you?" He held both palms up. "I tried to be very careful."

She bit her lip and shook her head. He had been very careful. Recalling her uncle's confidence in her, she forced herself to relax. Before Urokotori returned, Ebby needed to acclimate herself to being around this human and practice keeping herself under control. But the thought of embracing him for the swim made her heart beat hard and fast.

Get it together, she thought, settling to the sand as far from him as she could. "Will you tell me about humans?"

They spent the rest of the night talking, and by daybreak, she'd grown quite proficient at sign language. Her eyes were bleary from lack of sleep, but her heart felt strangely giddy and alive at the same time. By midmorning, Urokotori had not arrived, and Ebby's middle was a pit of hunger. Cruz's stomach rumbled in agreement. For all she knew, the other mermaid might never return. She had to go out for food.

Selecting a silver bracelet from her chest, she scoured it shiny with sand and approached Timuri. The octopus was quite intelligent in a foreign way and could transmit a message to Urokotori. Ebby wished she could bribe him to allow the human to pass, but a pet could never break a mistress's command, even at the cost of his life. She held out the bracelet. "Tell Urokotori this is for the human. For another day."

Timuri uncoiled one arm and Ebby slipped the bracelet over the tip. He withdrew it, tucking the jewelry away beneath him.

Ebby looked back into the cave at Cruz. "I'll be back soon with food."

"Take me with you." He floated expectantly in the middle of the cave.

"I can't." She'd imagined all the ways she might subvert Urokotori's order, but the mermaid had been very clear in her command. *Prevent the human from leaving the cave.* "You will be safe until I get back."

She hurried away, hoping that last statement was true.

*C*ruz drifted back and forth at the back of the cave, leaving glowing imprints each time he pushed gently off the wall. If he didn't get out of here soon he'd go stir crazy before the mermaids even got around to torturing him to death. Ebby'd said she'd be back soon, but that could mean anything in mermaid terms.

He was just finishing his umpteenth circuit of the small cave when a curvaceous shadow blocked the light from the doorway. *Finally!*

He turned, expecting Ebby, and found himself face-to-face with a familiar, freckled face and purple hair. She was singing, making come-hither movements with her fingers.

Biting his bottom lip, Cruz recalled Ebby's warning that he mustn't let the mermaids know he was not compelled.

But moving forward might be akin to sticking his head inside a hungry shark's mouth. He edged closer, playing the clumsy swimmer to buy him some time. Although she was smiling, her wicked teeth gleamed in the cavern's bioluminescent light. The all-too-familiar genital slit on her front looked swollen and pulsing. His heart thundered as he tried to read her intent. Playful or hungry?

Either option was equally unappealing.

As soon as he was within range, the mermaid reached beneath his kilt and grabbed his dick. None too gently, either.

She yanked him close and smashed her mouth against his, the sharp points of her teeth cutting into his lips. Attempting to accommodate her, he opened his mouth and kissed her back, swiping his tongue between her needle-like teeth. He reached up and pinched her nipple, working through his mind all the steps he might take to please a woman. His skin crawled everywhere it contacted hers, from her hungry lips to her hand on his cock demanding more than he wanted to give.

She thrust against him, hand firmly at the base of his shaft. Although he had a mild erection, he wasn't hard enough to enter her, and her thrashing grew more and more frenzied.

After a few fruitless minutes, she shoved him away, her face no longer remotely attractive. She bared her teeth in a snarl then opened her mouth wide. The cave's phytoplankton became blindingly bright, and the water seemed to shudder all around him.

He licked his lips, tasting blood, and moved forward, unsure what she might be commanding.

Obviously not sex, because she shoved him away again with a hard punch to his chest. He sailed backward, colliding with the wall hard enough to knock the breath from him.

The mermaid whirled and departed the cave in a flurry of sand.

Cruz pushed off the wall and choked on a mouthful of water. His lungs constricted in panic.

Remain calm. His years of diving experience kicked in. He opened his mouth to sip another breath like he would from a regulator when diving. Water rushed over his teeth, salting his tongue.

The breath-spell was gone.

9

*E*bby had just placed the last succulent frond of seaweed in a shell bowl when a familiar, purple-tailed shadow swept overhead. Selachii circled back, her freckled face etched with disgust. "I can't believe you actually paid to keep that human alive. He's all used up. Ugh."

Imagining the other mermaid rubbing herself over him made nausea rise in Ebby's throat. How did Selachii know about the deal? *Depths!* Had Urokotori returned to the cave while she was gone? Was she still there? Clutching the seaweed shell tighter, she asked, "Is Urokotori there?"

"She wasn't when I left. But I can see why." Selachii flipped a lock of hair out of her face and smoothed her hand down her flank as if brushing off some invisible sand. Her triggerfish skittered up to clean the area. "He couldn't even get it up." The mermaid cackled. "Your boringness must've rubbed off on him."

Ebby turned away. "Like I care. Why don't you go find some sea lions to torture and leave me alone?"

"Good idea." Selachii clapped her hands. "You should come along."

Although her heart was skipping beats, Ebby didn't bother to answer, pretending to continue her harvesting.

"So boring," Selachii kicked pebbles toward Ebby as she darted away.

The moment the purple fins had faded into the murky depths, Ebby dropped her shell and raced to the cave. Was she already too late? Jetting past the startled Timuri, she burst into the cave to find Cruz floating belly-up against the cave's ceiling. She cried out, sending the phytoplankton into a frenzy of brilliance.

Cruz turned his head to look at her.

A wash of relief sank her to the sandy floor. He was alive. She didn't even care that he'd been with Selachii, as long as he wasn't hurt.

He signed, "I can't breathe."

Her gut clenched when she saw air bubbles leak from his nose. A glance at the ceiling told her he'd been hanging onto life by gasping pockets of air trapped against the cave's solid stone. He wouldn't survive long on those.

She had to renew the breath-spell.

Her insides quivered. The briefest touch of his hand made her nervous. How was she going to handle the intimacy of a breath kiss? Would her mermaid instincts overcome her?

It didn't matter. There was no time to lose.

Before she could second-guess herself, she tore him from the ceiling, pulled his face to hers, and planted a chaste kiss on his lips before darting away.

He convulsed and stuffed his face back against the ceiling.

She'd never given a breath-spell before and wasn't sure how it worked, but apparently merely touching their lips together didn't do it.

Depths.

Steeling herself, she moved forward again. This time she pulled him into a full embrace, locking her lips against his. His arms wrapped around her shoulders in desperation, as if he could suck air from her through the kiss. Maybe that was it. She parted her lips and released a stream of bubbles into his mouth.

His chest swelled beneath her embrace. He slipped one hand around to the small of her back, holding her close. The stubble above his lip tickled her mouth, and she became aware of the way their bodies seemed to align in all the right places. The hard plane of his abs against her softer belly. His bare chest against her breasts, the fine mist of hair tickling her nipples. He was breathing now, yet seemed reluctant to let go.

And then she felt his tongue touch hers. The contact shot straight through her as if he was kissing her in places other than just her mouth. The hand on her back roamed up her spine, and he threaded his fingers into the hair at the base of her neck, guiding her head to deepen the kiss, drawing her tongue forward to tangle with his.

Indescribable pleasure shot through her like a drug. She let out a moan and sucked on his tongue. He shuddered, arms crushing her against his hard frame.

She ran one hand across the stubble on his jaw and

around his ear to the hard cords at the back of his neck. By Neptune, she'd never imagined a kiss could claim her so completely. Was this a side effect of the breath-spell? Her other hand traced the sleek muscles along his ribcage and up around a broad shoulder.

His lips moved against hers as if he could devour her, his arms holding her close. She hadn't seduced him with a song, and even if she'd tried, he was immune. Yet he wanted her.

He definitely wanted her.

His erection had grown between them. A gentle roll of her hips over the long, hard line caused him to moan into her mouth. The only thing blocking him from her slit was the thin silk kilt he wore around his hips. How easy it would be to lift it. To pull him free. To thrust herself forward and fill herself with his heat.

His hands swept down to cup her backside and grind against her, erection pulsing against her opening. Her core tensed with anticipation. What would he feel like inside her? Rubbing the deepest part of her. Filling her again and again. She wanted to open to him more than she'd ever wanted anything in her life. She wanted him to know her.

I need to stop this before things go any further.

She pulled away stiffly, reluctant to relinquish his touch.

His eyes were dilated, his fingertips slipping away from her skin with longing. Blinking once, he signed, "Thank you."

Ebby licked her kiss-swollen lips and nodded. "I'm sorry."

"For what?"

"I never considered Selachii a threat."

"Selachii is the purple mermaid?"

She nodded. Leaving him in here alone again wasn't an option unless she bought off all three mermaids, and she didn't have enough jewelry for that, not to mention it was only a temporary fix. She had to come up with a means to get him past Timuri and back on dry land.

Her hand went to the dart earring Lutana had given her. No, she'd already rejected that idea. Killing Timuri would be unforgivable. But what about commanding him? Mermaids were seldom able to exert control over a rival's pet, but Ebby had something Urokotori didn't—her mother's fish harp. Using the

A MERMAID'S HEART

stronger harp, Ebby's command spell might overcome Urokotori's.

Sensing her agitation, Kato shook himself free of sand and crouched over the harp's hiding spot. She knelt next to him, lifting him in her palm to face level. "Don't worry, dear friend. I don't want a new pet."

His antennae waved in agitation.

She set him down and gently excavated the delicate harp. Commanding Timuri would require strong magic, and there was bound to be trial and error as she honed her skill. Despite its small size, the harp weighed heavy in her grip as she turned toward the cave exit.

Cruz's attention moved from her face to her hand and back. "I thought you said she could never have that."

"It's not for her." Ebby swallowed tightly. "I'm going to use it."

"Can I help?"

She realized then that she would need to stay close to Timuri to maintain control and move him far enough away for Cruz to escape. The human was going to have to swim for the surface on his own. Pulling her dart earring free, she held it out to him. Once he'd taken it,

85

she clumsily signed one-handed, "This will kill a mermaid, but only use it as a last resort. The surface is far, and there are more mermaids than you have darts." She told him the rest of her plan. "I'll catch up to you once you're clear of the cave and make sure you reach land. Swim as fast as you can."

He set aside the dart and reached for the sea harp. She jerked it out of reach. He signed, "Let me put it on your necklace so you don't drop it."

She'd forgotten she wore the chain. Relinquishing her hold, she allowed him to unfasten the chain's clasp. His fingers brushing her skin made her shiver. Within moments, he'd slipped the golden strand through one of the many small holes in the harp's spine and returned the necklace to her throat. The small instrument weighed almost nothing, yet felt like a lead weight around her neck.

"Ready?" she asked.

He nodded.

Squaring her shoulders, she moved toward the entrance just as a sleek red form blocked the light.

Urokotori put her hands on her hips and raked her gaze over Cruz. "Selachii, you said the human was dead."

Ebby covered the harp with one palm. Urokotori had nearly killed Selachii in a battle over the small fish harp the red mermaid now owned. What would she do to get her hands on a larger, more powerful harp?

Selachii's voice drifted through the water from somewhere behind Urokotori. "He's not dead?"

"Our little prawn has decided to save him." Urokotori's fingertips drummed against her hips. "What do you find so fascinating about him, Ebby, if you're not going to fuck him?"

"I don't understand." Selachii's face appeared over Urokotori's shoulder. Her purple eyebrows furrowed.

Ebby moved in front of Cruz. "I want to buy his freedom. For real this time—as in alive and returned to dry land."

Urokotori shook her head, her face masked with disappointment. "You should never have chosen to be female, Ebby. You're just not up to the task."

"What do you care if I am or not?"

Dropping her hands from her hips, Urokotori pointed a long, clawed finger into the cave, her hair writhing around her like seagrass. "I'm growing tired of this game, little sister. You will become a true mermaid today."

Ebby's heartbeat thrummed loudly in her ears. "You can't make me."

An evil grin thinned Urokotori's crimson lips. "Oh, really? That sounds like a fun challenge." She tilted her head to one side. "I'll make you a deal. Seduce him before nightfall and I will let him out of the cave."

"If he can be seduced," Selachii joined in. "When I was here earlier, he was useless."

Urokotori's laughter rebounded off the cave walls. "A challenge for our little sister, then. If she fails, we'll give the human to Timuri."

"No!" Ebby pressed the fish harp until the tines dug into her chest. If only mermaid song worked against other mermaids; she'd have no qualms about commanding these two to kill each other. But killing wasn't the answer. Was seduction? Would giving up her virginity be so bad if it saved Cruz's life? *What if you become like Urokotori? Like Mother?* Her insides trembled at the thought.

"Fuck him and get it out of your system," Urokotori crooned. "I'm doing this for your own good." She lifted her two-pronged fish harp from where it dangled between her breasts and plucked a tine. A single note quivered through the water. "Earn his freedom."

Both of the other mermaids sidled backward a couple of yards and began to sing.

*C*ruz had no idea what was going on between Ebby and the other mermaids, but he knew it wasn't good. When the red mermaid lifted the turkey wishbone from the cord around her neck, he recognized it for what it was—a smaller version of Ebby's harp. He looked at Ebby, expecting her to use her larger harp to fend the mermaid off, but Ebby remained rigid, one hand clutching the harp pendant so tightly, he worried she'd crush the instrument.

Red-tail opened her mouth in what had to be a siren song, her clawed fingers plucking her harp.

Still, Ebby remained frozen.

Was red-tail using magic to paralyze her? The tiny dart was still in his hand, but there were two mermaids plus the lurking octopus. Reaching out with tentative fingers, he encircled Ebby's elbow and turned her to face him.

Her eyes were wide, her bottom lip caught between her teeth. She signed, "They're singing a seduction song."

Not paralyzed, then, at least not by magic. But she was afraid. Without turning his head, he glanced from the corner of his eye toward the entrance. "Can you counter their spell using your harp? It's bigger than Red-tail's."

"Harps don't work on other mermaids. Their song is supposed to work on you."

Her words settled over him like scuba-diving weights. All the admonishments not to touch her, and now she was supposed to have sex with him? Not that he didn't want her, but...

She took his free hand and placed it on one of her breasts. The nipple hardened beneath his palm, but he knew from experience that just because the body responded didn't mean someone was aroused. He pulled it away and signed, "Should we use the dart?"

A sad smile lifted one corner of her mouth and she shook her head. "It wouldn't be enough. They said that after I seduce you, they'll set you free."

Despite his hesitation, his dick hardened at her words. The kiss they'd shared when she restored his breath-spell had been amazing. The way her mouth had tasted of amber and musk, reminding him of an ocean at sunset. How warm she'd felt against his body.

She reached out and placed his palm on her breast again, sliding close until her lips were within inches of his. The hand cupping her breast was now trapped between them. His dick jumped to full attention. Perhaps he was immune to mermaid songs, but he was definitely still affected by her.

Taking the lead, he brushed his lips over hers. He wanted this. Wanted her—more than he'd ever wanted anyone, captivity be damned. At least if he died, he'd die happy.

She opened her mouth, back arching slightly as she accepted his kiss. Her tongue played over his lower lip and her nipple hardened beneath his palm.

Worried he might accidentally jab her with the dart, he let it slip from his fingers and stroked his hand over the smooth skin at the small of her back. She was so warm and pliable, the tiny dimples above what would be her ass making his dick harden even more. He wanted to explore every inch of her. Pulling her hips close to his, he claimed her mouth in a full, deep kiss.

She tangled her tongue with his while her fingers dug into his hair. If he'd thought the breath kiss had been magic, then this was nirvana. And Ebby was his goddess.

10

*E*bby'd always assumed the mermaids did all the seducing, but Cruz was doing a pretty good job of it himself. His hands kneaded her backside, rubbing her against the heat of his erection, while his tongue plunged in and out of her mouth, a sex act all its own. One big palm slid up her back and gripped her hair, forcing her head back, and he left her mouth to trail his stubbled chin lightly down her neck, nipping and sucking her tender skin and giving her sparks of delight.

She ran her hands over his chest, intrigued by his hair. Humans had so much hair! His small nipples hardened to pinpoints under her fingertips, the defined curve of his pecs flexing as he adjusted his grip around her waist.

Depths, he was a beautiful man. She suddenly wanted to see him. All of him. Close.

She gently walked her hands down his torso until she knelt on her tail fin, at eye level with the silk covering his throbbing erection. His hands remained tangled in her hair and his muscular legs spread wide, adjusting to keep him upright in the water. She ran her palms up his rock-hard thighs, enjoying the feel of his coarse hair as she pushed the silk aside. When she reached his balls, she cupped them, rolling them gently beneath her fingers. The fragile softness there contrasted completely with the hard shaft pulsing in response to her attention.

She gripped his base, squeezing and pulling until a milky bead appeared at the tip. A delighted shudder ran through her at his response. She'd never been this close to a man before, though she'd seen the way their bodies reacted during her many spying sessions. Experiencing his reaction was even better than she'd imagined.

His herbal scent filled the water as she swept her tongue across the head of his cock then plunged his thick length into her mouth. Under her tongue, his ridges and heat provided a whole new sensation, and she wanted more. Wrapping her lips over her teeth to protect him, she took as much of him inside her as she could, jaw aching as she sucked and pulled.

His hands caressed her scalp, urging her to meet the rhythm of his flexing hips. She wrapped her hands around his ass, sliding her fingers down to feel where his legs split. He seemed to like that, so she explored with her fingertips while her mouth conquered his length. Soon, he was quivering, ass flexed and thigh muscles hard as rocks. She sucked harder. But instead of exploding as she expected, he shuddered and pushed her away.

Was he done? Disappointment squeezed her chest. That wasn't at all what she'd expected.

She tilted her face up. His hazel eyes were dark with desire and his chest heaved. Smiling, he signed, "Slow down."

Thank Neptune he wasn't done. Remembering the other mermaids watching, she glanced at them. They continued singing, sharp gazes possibly as hungry for climax as she was.

Cruz sank to his knees and dipped his head to her breast, once again surrounding her in the moment. The stubble on his chin seared a mark across her heart. When his tongue swirled around her nipple, her back arched as if lightning had hit her belly button. *Ah, Neptune, what delightful torture!*

Wrapping her fingers into his hair, she arched again, offering up her other breast. He nipped and sucked and teased until she wondered how she could stand one second more. A heat was building deep in her core. Her primal-self ached for one thing. One hard, thick thing.

Ebby stretched one hand downward, seeking his erection once more. But Cruz slid down her body, angling his cock farther away and trailing his mouth along her abdomen toward the sleek skin where her pulsing slit waited. She whimpered, frustrated yet delighted at the new sensation. His fingers massaged her backside, pulling her hips ever closer to his mouth until his tongue flicked out and entered the top of her opening. That brief contact sent a ripple through her and she flexed, desperate for more.

He obliged, tangling his tongue around the nub of her pleasure. *Depths.* She'd touched herself many times but never had it felt this good. Sucking and prodding, he penetrated her with his tongue, driving her wild. She bucked against him, ripple after ripple of pleasure running from her scalp to her fins.

Their activity had driven her backward into the cave wall, igniting a fury of teal-green light. The rough stone against her back only heightened her arousal, and she pulled him closer, wanting, wanting... His finger joined his tongue, finding her opening and pressing past her folds.

She exploded around him, the calloused pad of his finger deep within her. She'd experienced orgasm before, but under the control of another person, the sensation was mind-blowing.

He continued stroking until she'd finished shuddering. Withdrawing slowly, he pulled himself up the length of her body, his skin sliding along hers somehow raising her to new levels of desire. His mouth had been fabulous, his finger divine, but still, she wanted more. She wanted all of him.

Slipping a hand between them, she gripped the base of his shaft, guiding him to her entrance. He paused his kiss and pulled back just enough to meet her gaze. *I want you*, she thought, willing him with her eyes.

And he understood. He thrust forward, penetrating her. Opening her. Filling her.

Again and again he thrust, driving her against the cave wall, filling the water with tiny motes of bioluminescent light as phytoplankton dislodged and floated free. The heat of his body melding into hers seemed to be more than physical. More than primal. It was a spiritual thing, a thing above all others, and for the first time she thought she understood why the other mermaids were so driven to perform this act again and again.

It felt as if he *knew* her. As if he had access to every deep dark secret and lofty wish.

She never wanted it to end. Never wanted to be apart. She gripped him tightly, letting wave after wave break over her until her climax shattered her into a million pieces.

At nearly the same moment, he seated himself inside her with a final thrust, his hot seed shooting directly into her core and drawing from her one final shudder of ecstasy.

He kept a tight hold on her as she trembled, his warmth seeping into her, filling her, consuming her. Her head swam with thoughts and emotions as if she was unsure where she ended and Cruz began. Images flashed behind her eyes, lights, faces—things she didn't understand. And then out of the mist rose a coherent sentence. *That was some orgasm. How can a fish be so damned hot?*

Inside, she laughed. *I'm not a fish.* She would never think of herself as a fish. Then the satisfaction in her heart cooled as she realized what was happening. Sometimes a merman would bond to a mermaid so fiercely it allowed her to hear his thoughts. Such bonds were prized by mermaids because it gave them even greater control of their helpless mates. She had no idea humans were also susceptible.

His thoughts were content. Languid. His hands crept down to cup her backside. *Not a fish. A mythological creature. A woman.* He pulled her tightly against him. *My mythological woman.*

Despite her dismay that he was now under her power, a bubble of laughter filled her chest. He was as delightful in his head as he was with his hand language. More so, even. If only the connection wasn't one-way. She ran her fingertips over his stubbled cheek. *I wish you could hear me, Cruz.*

His lashes fluttered open to meet her gaze, his irises still dark with lust. *Get a grip on yourself, Cruz. You can't hear her thoughts.*

She frowned, her wish igniting into something closer to dread. Had he just said he could hear her?

His attention shifted to her mouth. *What's going on? I swear she's talking to me. Can mermaid magic restore hearing?*

Full-blown panic took hold of Ebby and she pushed him away. She could hear him—rare enough—but if he could hear her in return... *The mate bond.* No, it couldn't be. She was a mermaid. She should be immune to the mate-bond. Carefully, she crafted her next thought. *Cruz, can you hear me?*

He blinked slowly, his eyebrows pinching together, and nodded. *Is this more mermaid magic?*

The array of emotions passing through her threatened to make her pass out. She recalled the trips to the Deeps she'd taken with Da, where she'd heard the ancient blue whales sing of true mates and lost magic. *Something stronger. Only true mates can hear each other.*

True mates? He cocked his head again, raising his brows. He seemed to be taking this head-talking thing in stride.

Ebby wasn't. She'd become a mermaid to avoid the shackle of a mate bond. Mate bonds only caused heartache and a slow, living death. She'd watched it consume her father. This couldn't be happening. It just wasn't possible. She backed away in horror, arms raised to keep him away.

Cruz reached for her, eyebrows puckered with concern. *Ebby?*

She couldn't allow him to touch her again and incite her desire. Not when the unfathomable had just happened. The word *trapped* kept cycling through her mind. Spinning, Ebby shot from the cave and past the other mermaids, Cruz's voice calling her name in her head.

Laughter resonated through the water behind her, drowning out Cruz's words.

"We told you you'd see the light, sister!" Urokotori's voice twisted Ebby's confusion into fury.

Whipping around, Ebby found herself face to face with Selachii. Lightning quick, the purple-tailed mermaid snapped the chain from Ebby's neck, enveloping the attached fish harp in one clawed hand.

Ebby lunged for it, but Selachii's triggerfish snapped its powerful jaws, almost taking off her finger. New terror took root inside Ebby's chest. "Give that back."

Selachii strummed the tines, eliciting a mesmerizing note that sent Ebby flashing back to her mother. That harp had announced her mother's arrival every time she visited Da's nest, driving Ebby into hiding for the duration of her visit.

"Where did you get this, dear sister?" Selachii crooned in harmony with the harp.

The triggerfish circled Selachii's hips as if doing a victory dance.

"It's my mother's," Ebby grit through her teeth. How foolish she'd been, bringing the harp into the open.

Urokotori drifted to a halt beside her purple-tailed sister, eyes narrowed. "Let me see it."

Selachii bared her teeth at the red-tailed mermaid. "Don't think for one second you can force me to hand it over like you did last time." She eyed the one hanging around Urokotori's neck before brandishing the one she held. "This one's got nine tines."

"It's not the size of the instrument." Urokotori flicked a lock of hair over her shoulder and tossed her chin. Her gaze never wavered from the tines poking like grotesque fingers from Selachii's grip. "It's how you play it that counts. You're going to need a lot of practice."

Selachii let out an offended screech, her purple hair fanning out around her head like a puffer fish. She hesitated a heartbeat, as if considering a frontal attack, then jerked around and darted through the kelp, her triggerfish close on her fins.

"Wait!" Ebby cried, flexing her tail muscles to follow.

Strong, clawed hands trapped her wrist, jerking her to Urokotori's side. "Oh, no you don't. It's time to put an end to your childish resistance once and for all."

The larger mermaid took off in the opposite direction, grip tight enough to make Ebby's arm feel as though it might rip from its socket.

Balling her other hand into a fist, Ebby slammed it into Urokotori's kidney. The other mermaid grunted, her hold loosening. Ebby ripped herself free, swimming back toward the cave.

Urokotori plucked a tine on her harp, and a cluster of yellow-bellied sea snakes darted upward from the rocks, intercepting Ebby's course. They coiled their tails tightly around Ebby's throat and arms. One venomous beast stared her in the eye with fangs bared.

Ebby froze, letting the current carry her stiffly back toward Urokotori. Sea snakes were generally not aggressive, but under a mermaid's command, they became the deadliest creature in the entire ocean.

Urokotori laced her fingers through Ebby's as if they were the best of friends and led her onward. "You're pathetic. You could've been the most powerful mermaid in the sea with that harp. It's completely wasted on that idiot Selachii."

Ebby hooked her tail fin on rocks and coral, hoping to create some drag. "You're not going to let her keep it, are you?"

"Of course not," Urokotori yanked on her arm. "Once you're secure, I'll take care of her."

"Secure? What are you talking about?"

"You'll see."

Ahead, the jutting mast of the slave ship pierced the faint blades of sunlight bisecting the current. The pit of Ebby's stomach grew ice cold. Years ago, she'd been horrified by the bones in the human ship, arms and legs still attached to heavy chains within the hold. Her father had bypassed the gory spaces, sifting through the upper levels where the crew had stayed. But the memory of all those helpless humans had remained with Ebby.

Urokotori dragged her over the bow of the ship toward the hatch.

"Let me go. We have more important things to do. Like get that harp back before Selachii figures out how to use it." Ebby didn't like the idea of Urokotori getting her hands on the instrument, either, but at this point, any distraction would be useful. "You don't want her to be stronger than you are, do you?"

Seemingly deaf to Ebby's words, Urokotori shoved her into a hallway, following it lower into the dark recesses of the ship. No light penetrated the underbelly, but Ebby's mermaid gaze could see enough to know the skeletons were just as she remembered. A fine filter of sediment covered the remains, but the outlines of human bodies were clear. Row upon row of the dead, chained to the floor of the hold as the water flooded in, unable to escape, unable to break the bonds that held them down.

The sea snakes were growing agitated, tails tightening around Ebby's throat. Any sudden move could get her killed. A hum built low in her throat, instinct telling her to at least attempt to countermand Urokotori's hold on the creatures. Without a harp, she stood little chance, but her proximity to the snakes might give her a small advantage. She'd just opened her mouth to utter her directive when a cold weight settled around her wrist.

"There," Urokotori said. "I've always wanted to do that."

A heavy iron cuff chafed Ebby's skin, connected to the grisly floorboards by a thick chain.

Urokotori clicked her tongue, freeing the snakes from her charm. They let go and wriggled away. Ebby jerked ineffectually against the chain, the metal links grating and clunking against each other. "What are you doing?" The rusty manacle was securely locked around her wrist. "Do you even have a key for this?"

Urokotori waved an unconcerned hand. "I'm sure there's one around here somewhere. Once you've learned your lesson, I'll track it down."

"What lesson?" Ebby recalled the trips with her father and the detritus scattered around the ship's cabins. Finding a key would be next to impossible.

"Don't worry. I'll be back with your pathetic human." Urokotori pushed herself toward the hatch.

Ebby jerked her wrist again, rough iron biting into her skin. "No! You said you'd set him free!"

Urokotori turned, a dark silhouette within the hold's deep shadows. "I said I'd let him out of the cave. What do you find so appealing about that male, anyway?" Without giving Ebby a chance to respond, the mermaid spun and exited the hold. Her voice floated back through the corridor. "Not that it matters. You'll see how fragile humans are once I've finished with him."

"Come back! Don't leave me here!"

Only the thrum of the ever-pressing current against the ship's hull responded.

11

*C*ruz paced the cave a safe distance away from the octopus guarding the exit. Confusion was tearing him apart. Ebby's voice inside his mind had been the most intimate thing he'd ever experienced, even more gratifying than sex in a way, and her sudden departure had cut him to the quick. Did he sound as stupid in her head as he did when he spoke aloud? People had been rude to him lots of times, making fun of his impairment, but he didn't think he'd ever put off anyone badly enough to drive them away.

This entire situation was fucked as hell. Why had Ebby run away? She seemed to think he was her true mate, but he didn't know enough about mermaids to know what that meant or even make a guess about her true motives.

For all he knew, she'd been able to hear his thoughts all along. Maybe that's how she'd figured out sign language so quickly. *Shit*. Had she lied to him this whole time? It hadn't felt like she was lying to him. Maybe she'd been right and losing her virginity really did change her into a man-eating monster like the others. Yet obviously Ebby would rather flee than hurt him.

So maybe she wasn't a monster?

He shook his head and ran his fingertips over the dart, careful not to prick himself on the sharp point. Ebby's mantis shrimp had helped him locate the ivory sliver. If the poison was strong enough to kill a mermaid, would it kill an octopus? He glanced at the entrance again. He'd need to get close enough to do it.

Edging forward with the dart in one hand, he watched the octopus watching him and remembered the searing blow it had delivered last time he'd come too close. What if it killed him this time? *Fuck*. No way he could dart the animal before it knocked him senseless. He threaded the dart into the hem of his makeshift kilt. What a useless weapon. All he could do was wait for Ebby—or one of the others—to return.

When a female figure finally blocked the light at the entrance, Cruz forced himself to keep his hand away from the dart. If it was Ebby, he didn't want to hurt her accidentally, and if it was one of the others, he needed to somehow get out of the cave before he struck, or he'd only succeed in becoming trapped with a dead mermaid.

Blue filtered sunlight illuminated the mermaid's tail fin as if it was purple tissue paper. The mermaid who'd stolen his breath. His heartbeat increased as she slithered into the cave followed by a huge triggerfish. Was she singing to control him? He had to assume she was.

Pretending to be under her spell, he floundered toward her until he was close enough to see her face. Her amethyst eyes assessed him, lips parted provocatively. Then she lifted her hands, and he saw the gold-tipped prongs of a harp with one missing tine. *That's Ebby's.* Dread tightened his chest. She'd been very clear the others mustn't get their hands on the instrument. If this mermaid now carried it, then Ebby must be in trouble.

Or dead. He shook the idea out of his head, refusing to believe it. He didn't want to think of her as gone.

The purple-tailed mermaid ran her fingers over the tines, and the cavern lights flared in response. He could only imagine the sound reverberating off the walls. Although he couldn't hear, the vibrations were strong enough to cause an uncomfortable stirring in his groin. Ebby'd said it would amplify a mermaid's power, and it seemed to be working even despite his deafness.

He swallowed thickly and moved within range of her arms. The triggerfish zipped back and forth at her shoulder, toothed mouth snapping. Now wasn't the time to worry about the song or the harp. He was trapped in here unless he could convince her to take him outside. Hating to expose himself, he reached down and lifted the fabric, stroking his shaft into forced readiness. With his other hand, he pointed outside.

She grinned and reached for him.

He pointed toward the exit once more and tried to pull off a seductive smolder with his gaze.

She seemed to consider, eyes taking in the cave with distaste. Then her smile widened as if she'd realized something. Looking over her shoulder, she fluttered her fingertips over the harp.

The octopus swelled, then shuddered before withdrawing from sight. The triggerfish spun in frenzied circles around the mermaid as if performing a victory dance.

The mermaid turned her attention once more toward Cruz, her eyes feverishly alight. She held out a clawed hand as if in invitation.

Cruz's heart threatened to stampede out of the cave ahead of him. *Patience.* He couldn't be sure the octopus was gone. Keeping up his pretended desire, he took her hand. He'd have to be close to use the dart, anyway. Once they were clear of the cave, he'd stab her and make his escape.

In a sudden, snake-like move, she pulled him against her and swept them both into the filtered light. Coral and stones swept by with dizzying speed.

After a few moments, her grip loosened enough for him to get his bearings. Her clawed hands cupped his face, her lips pursed for a kiss, and pulled him toward her expectantly.

Cruz fumbled with the hem of his kilt, feeling carefully for the splinter of the dart woven into it. Where was that damned thing? The mermaid shoved her mouth against his, tongue forcing itself between his lips. Her claws dug painfully into his cheeks, but he forced himself to remain compliant, using one hand to pinch her nipple while his other continued to search the edge of the silk.

There. Her tail thrashed the water, hips thrusting against his as the violent kiss threatened to shred his lips. If he wasn't careful, he'd drop the dart. Or worse, poke himself. Did he actually have to jab it into her or would a scratch be enough? He couldn't risk failure. Yanking the dart free, he jabbed the sharp point into her waist.

The mermaid's body stiffened. She twisted to look at her waist, claws fumbling at the protruding dart. Yanking it free in a cloud of blood, she turned her furious gaze back to him and tightened her grip on his forearm.

His stomach dropped to the sea floor. *It didn't work.* All he'd done was make her angry. He braced himself to receive her killing blow.

Suddenly, her back arched and her grip clamped down like a shark's bite. She opened her mouth wide, exposing razor-sharp teeth. He threw up an arm to shield himself. But instead of teeth, her tail slammed into his ribs with a force that knocked the breath from his body. Still caught in her grip, Cruz was thrown into a wild downward spin. He lost all sense of up or down as they plummeted past a wall of rocks and coral. Stones scraped his shoulder. Bruised his knee. He pried at her grip on his arm until they hit the bottom with numbing force.

The impact broke her hold, and he gulped grateful breaths of water while the mermaid continued convulsing, stirring up a cloud of debris. With a final arch of her back, she settled to the sea floor, eyes staring sightlessly toward the shifting pattern of sunlit ripples high above. Around her neck, the gold tines of the harp caught the light, sparkling through the settling haze.

Was she really dead? Much as he needed to kick toward the surface, he forced himself to approach her body. Her tail quivered, but her slack face gave him courage. Broken tines lay scattered on the sea floor around her, but on the chain around her neck, the harp's spine still bore two golden prongs. He reached for the instrument. Was it still as powerful as Ebby claimed? The chain's clasp was broken, and the mermaid had tied the gold links into a knot behind her neck. Her purple hair had tangled in the chain, but he broke it free.

Nervous she might revive, he backed away. She remained lifeless, sand settling over her skin.

Rising from the carnage on the sea floor, he looked around. The purple mermaid's fall had dropped him into a gulley between coral-studded rock walls. He was reminded of another time he'd climbed from a ravine, leaving behind a crushed vehicle with his mother inside. He clutched the harp tighter in one fist. If Ebby'd lost this, it meant she was in trouble.

He wouldn't leave until he knew she was safe. She'd stood up for him when the other mermaids wanted to rip him apart. She'd fed him, taken the time to learn sign language, and even given him her virginity. Her parting words about being true mates had him kicking upward, surveying the wall to get his bearings. Part of him seemed to think the purple mermaid had swum up the current with him, but he couldn't be sure.

He gazed down current. Going back might be dangerous, but Ebby's pet shrimp was still there and might know how to find her.

He struck out across the current toward the kelp a short distance away, planning to use it as cover while he paralleled the wall. His arm ached where the mermaid's claws had drawn blood, but there wasn't enough spilling into the water to concern him about sharks. Half swimming and half pushing against the slippery kelp stalks, he wove through the forest, keeping sight of the wall through the gaps between the fronds. Small fish darted away at his approach, flashing silver and teal and orange in the shafts of sunlight. How far was he below the surface? It felt odd to be swimming this deep without any gear to weigh him down. He pulled in a breath, marveling again at how easy it was. How long would the spell last?

A darker spot on the wall caught his attention, and he paused, treading water and peeking through the swaying leaves. It looked like the cave he'd been imprisoned in. Was the octopus still guarding it? Gripping a thick, slippery stalk, he looked closer. A flash of movement caught his eye on the sandy floor. His pulse thrummed loudly in his ears as eight boneless legs twisted and furled, propelling the beast toward the kelp.

For a brief moment, he wondered if it had spotted him, but then he noticed a small plume of sand that seemed to be leading the creature forward. Some sort of prey. The smaller plume settled without warning and the octopus paused. As the sand settled, Cruz realized it was a mantis shrimp. Ebby's pet must be trying to make his escape.

The octopus coiled itself, poised to pounce. The shrimp faced it on its hind legs like a boxer daring a bully to come closer, raptorial claws pulled tight against its chest.

He'd read that those claws could deliver a bullet-like punch strong enough to break glass, but would it be a match for a creature the size of an octopus? In short lunges, the octopus tested its prey. The shrimp stood its ground, back legs scurrying to keep it facing its enemy.

Cruz held tight to the kelp, unsure what to do. The shrimp hardly stood a chance, yet Cruz was no match for the octopus, either. His chest still felt bruised from being slammed back in the cave. But leaving Ebby's pet to be devoured seemed cruel. He glanced down at the sea floor, looking for something to throw before remembering how ineffective that would be under water. He still held the harp in his other hand; too bad he couldn't sing like a mermaid, or he'd just tell the octopus to back off.

He looked back up in time to see the shrimp jet toward the octopus in a motion almost too fast to see. All eight of the octopus's legs shot out straight and stiff. The shrimp appeared to ricochet off the larger creature's head, changing trajectory like a billiard ball and zooming straight toward the kelp. Behind it, the octopus sank stiffly to the floor.

Holy hell! Had that tiny shrimp just killed the octopus or only stunned it? He held aside a swaying frond, watching the octopus. A brief moment later, its legs curled back in and it woozily crawled back toward its cave.

Dropping toward the forest's knobby floor, Cruz moved down current searching for signs of Ebby's pet.

He found the little guy cowering in the midst of a group of spiny black sea urchins. Would it recognize him as a friend? He held out a hand like he'd seen Ebby do.

The creature waved its long antennae at him but stayed firmly entrenched between the poisonous spines.

He couldn't blame the guy. The only other times he'd hunted for crustaceans had been for an entirely different purpose. Maybe if he made it clear he meant no harm? He opened the hand holding the harp and held it out for the creature to see. Maybe a familiar object would convince it to come closer.

The shrimp shot forward, and Cruz flinched, expecting to end up like the octopus. The harp was wrenched from his fingertips. Pointed legs prickled along his arm toward his face, then settled on his shoulder. Cruz opened his eyes, shoulders relaxing as he realized the creature had settled in for a ride, harp clasped protectively between its claws.

Cruz smiled in relief and signed, "Any idea where to find Ebby, my friend?"

Tiny legs tickled his shoulder, and the creature adjusted itself to face down current.

Okay. Down current it was.

He pushed through the kelp, trying not to shrug off the tickle of the shrimp's feet against his shoulder. How did Ebby stand it? The current had already pushed him past the cave, and a short while later, the kelp forest ended. The sea floor dropped away at an abrupt edge.

Below, three masts of a shipwreck jutted upward like pointed teeth. On his shoulder, the shrimp jacked itself up and down on its hind legs, as if signaling him to go on.

Cruz tread water, looking at the open expanse before him. He was a strong swimmer, but without scuba gear, he'd be helpless against the currents and large predators found in open water, not to mention he'd no longer be hidden from potential mermaid eyes.

"She's in there? You sure?" he signed, looking at the shrimp.

The creature responded by launching off his shoulder, carrying the harp with it as it drifted down the rocky drop-off.

Sighing, Cruz followed, skimming the wall behind the shrimp. He hoped he wasn't reading too much into the shrimp's actions. For all he knew, this wasn't even Ebby's pet, and he was following some random creature to some random place. At least the current was assisting in pushing him toward the wreck. What if Ebby wasn't here? He didn't want to think of how he was going to overcome it to get back.

As he moved deeper toward the ship, the water got colder, and the light dimmed until all he could see was shadows of blue and green. His heart thundered against his ribs, and his muscles trembled with exertion and chill. What he wouldn't do for a few of the phytoplankton from the cave to light his way.

Below him, the shrimp disappeared between a small outcropping of rocks. Cruz swam past, taking a moment to realize it hadn't emerged again. Turning to see if the shrimp had changed direction, he froze, gaze lifting toward a sinuous shadow outlined in the light coming from the surface.

A mermaid floated a few arms lengths above him, her tail gyrating lazily, long hair fanned out like a halo. *Ebby?*

She dipped toward him.

In the dim light, her features resolved into crimson lips and a slow, predatory grin.

*E*bby pulled against the chain, the links rattling and clanking as she tried to jerk free again and again. Her wrist was throbbing and raw and blood scented the stale water inside the ship's hold, but sharks were the last thing on her mind.

She'd been calling Cruz, hoping to warn him for what felt like hours, but apparently, the mate bond connection was limited by distance. Why had she fled the cave? She'd not only lost the harp, she'd abandoned Cruz to the mercies of the other mermaids. Everything she'd done, everything she'd sacrificed, had been for nothing. She thought of his voice in her head, a connection she'd never dreamed of experiencing. She should have savored it, not run away. A mate bond was so rare it was almost impossible. And she'd squandered it.

A familiar song outside the ship grew stronger, the dulcet notes of Urokotori's seduction magic approaching. The other mermaid must be returning with Cruz already. Ebby's stomach roiled as she called yet again. *Cruz, can you hear me?*

His voice entered her mind, frantic and gasping. *Ebby? Ebby, where are you?*

He was alive! *Cruz! Do you have the dart? Use it now! Get away!*

I already used it on the purple mermaid. Cruz's voice was tight, as though he spoke through gritted teeth.

Nausea filled her. Was he hurt? She should've realized Selachii would want a test subject for her new harp. Then another horror struck her. If the purple mermaid was dead, that meant Urokotori had the harp. She would be unstoppable. Ebby twisted her hand, trying to unscrew it from the manacle until her bones ached.

From the hatch, a tentacled leg appeared, then another and another. Ebby drew back as Timuri boiled into the hold. He pulsed with angry color, but instead of attacking her, he pulled himself against the ceiling in the far corner to await his mistress's arrival. Urokotori wasn't far behind, towing Cruz along by one wrist. His other hand grappled uselessly against her grip. *Ebby, are you in here? I can barely see.*

I'm here. Ebby sang a wavering note that ignited the few sickly phytoplankton drifting inside the hold. The pale green bioluminescence made the fresh bruises and cuts marring his skin look terrible. *You're hurt!*

I'm okay. His tone belied his words.

"Your human somehow convinced Selachii to set him free." Urokotori shoved him toward her pet, who sullenly wrapped several legs around Cruz's limbs. "And he appears to be immune to my song."

Oh, no. If Urokotori knew he was deaf, there was no telling what she might do to torture him. *Why didn't you pretend to hear her?*

She came up behind me while I was looking for you.

The octopus jerked the flailing man toward its beak. Urokotori issued a command at the creature to halt. Beak clacking, the octopus quivered, obviously chafing against her control.

A diversion came to Ebby's mind. "You seem to be struggling with your pet, Urokotori. Maybe your song isn't as strong as you think."

The other mermaid rounded on her, jabbing a long, clawed finger her direction. "He's agitated because your pet attacked him!"

Ebby's throat tightened. She'd abandoned Kato in the cave along with Cruz. Although the little shrimp packed a big punch, she doubted he could hold his own against Timuri for long. Poor Kato had become a meal because of her. Grief blurred her vision with briny tears. It seemed everyone she loved was falling prey to Urokotori's whim. *Oh, Kato!*

Don't worry, Cruz soothed. *Your little shrimp clobbered the octopus and got away.*

A weak smile tugged at Ebby's mouth. Her mate was facing a horrible death, yet here he was comforting her. She raised her chin and glared at Urokotori. "It's not the size of the pet, but how you use it that counts."

Urokotori's upper lip curled into a snarl. "You want me to use my pet? Fine." She commanded Timuri to spread Cruz's limbs like a sacrifice.

Muscles bunching, Cruz released a growl that could rival a sea lion, jerked one hand free of the octopus's tentacle, and reached for Urokotori's throat.

She slipped backward with a delighted chuckle, sending the glowing phytoplankton swirling around her. "He's ready to play!"

"Leave him alone!" Ebby stretched at the end of her chain, her free hand inches from Urokotori's back. "I'll do whatever you want!"

Urokotori remained focused on Cruz's grimacing face while he flailed against the octopus's grip. "This is going to be fun."

He bared his blunt teeth at Urokotori, limbs quivering as she slid her tail fin upward between his legs. Urokotori trailed her claws down his chest to his navel. His six-pack bulged as he attempted to curl away from her touch.

Ebby's blood surged in her ears, every heartbeat a countdown to certain death. She had to protect her mate.

Her fingers brushed the ends of Urokotori's black hair. Straining against the manacle, she gained another centimeter. More hair threaded between her fingers. She curled her hand into a fist and yanked, snapping the other mermaid's head back.

Lightning quick, Ebby swept her tail up and smashed into Urokotori's back.

The other mermaid jackknifed, taking the hit against her tail, instead. She spun, leaving Ebby with a handful of hair, and raked her claws down Ebby's cheek. Blood misted the water.

Ebby curled her own claws and swiped at her opponent, catching the mermaid on the forearm.

Urokotori's crimson lips were slashes of fury against her pale face. "Finally found your spine, little sister?"

"Let me go and we'll battle this out fair and square." Ebby pulled on the chain, wondering how she could lure the other mermaid close enough to wrap it around her throat.

"You know I don't fight fair. I'll deal with you once I've finished my fun with your lover. I'm curious how pliable I can make him without the effect of a mer-song." With a swish of her red fins, she spun and slithered her body up Cruz's, her hands lifting his kilt.

Cruz's thoughts churned with helpless anger, fear, and indignation.

Ebby felt the same way. She scoured the floor around her for a weapon, a distraction, anything that might give Cruz a chance to escape. To her left, something moved beneath the broken floorboards. Kato pulled himself between a gap and scuttled toward her, little gills fluttering with effort. Two gold-tipped prongs jutted from his front claws like a moray eel's bottom teeth. *My harp?*

Bending quickly, she took the instrument. All but two tines had been snapped off, leaving jagged nubs along its base. She glanced at Urokotori, whose tail undulated as sinuously as a sea snake while she rubbed herself over Cruz's body, crooning a lurid description of her plans to milk his seed dry.

Was there enough power in the broken harp to negate Urokotori's magic? Timuri was already agitated, and Urokotori was occupied tormenting Cruz. If Ebby could break Urokotori's hold on the octopus and command him to release Cruz, the human might stand a chance. On the other hand, breaking the mermaid's control might free the monster to rip Cruz to pieces.

What other choice was there?

Swallowing hard, she brought the harp in front of her and gently stroked the tines, sending a quivering chord through the ship's hold. The phytoplankton seemed to brighten. She steadied her grasp on the instrument, adding her voice. She sang of peace and gentleness. Sunlight and sweet water.

Timuri's limbs rippled, coiled tips loosening. Cruz pulled his limbs free.

Urokotori twisted, gaping at Ebby. "How dare you!"

The tip of one suction-cupped arm curled over Urokotori's shoulder. She spun, strumming her smaller harp. Her practiced voice clamped down on the creature, forcing him to recoil in cringing submission.

What's happening? Cruz kicked through the water toward Ebby.

Ebby couldn't spare a thread of concentration to answer.

"Your human will suffer for this!" Urokotori poured anger into her song, commanding the octopus to rend and tear.

Timuri shuddered, beak opening and closing as the command songs overlapped.

129

Ebby pulled notes from deep in her chest, stroking the tines more firmly and countermanding the violence, trying to calm the beast. But years of conditioning had made the creature hostile. It's long arm snagged Cruz's ankle.

Urokotori laughed, alternating her dual notes in a chaotic melody that caused the surrounding phytoplankton to flicker. Timuri's skin rippled with frustrated colors, slitted gaze on his mistress even as he pulled Cruz toward his gaping beak. Ebby couldn't overcome the creature's nature. An octopus was designed to hunt and eat. Urokotori only had to encourage his instincts.

The answer came to Ebby like mid-morning light into a kelp clearing. It was time to stop fighting Urokotori's song.

Shifting her key, she sang of vengeance, complementing Urokotori's command for violence. Enhancing it.

And redirected it toward Urokotori.

The beast must've been waiting for the opportunity for years. In a flash, Timuri released Cruz and swelled in size, looming over the mistress who'd held him captive to her will for so long.

Urokotori's song went sour with panic.

In a flash of motion, all eight of the octopus's legs engulfed her, pulling her body inward. His hungry beak pierced her chest in an explosion of blood. Urokotori's screech cut short as the creature ripped her heart from her ribcage.

Fighting the urge to retch, Ebby gentled her command, asking the octopus to find a more secluded place to consume his meal.

Timuri shifted his grip on the mermaid's limp corpse, furled his other legs beneath him, and disappeared through the hatch.

*a*fter the cloudy water ceased churning, Cruz pulled himself from the clutter of broken barrels and crates. The red-tailed mermaid was no longer in sight. Only Ebby remained, her apricot tail and billowing auburn hair a beacon in the dim bioluminescent glow. Through their mental connection, her mind flowed like a riptide, her internal song both ferocious and melodic.

Cruz glanced toward the dark corners, checking for the red-tailed mermaid before darting forward and taking Ebby into his arms. *Ebby, you can stop. They've gone.*

Her song went silent, her eyes staring through him with blown pupils. *Oh, Neptune. I killed her.*

Ebby, it's okay. Crushing her against him, he felt her pain as if it was his own, yet he was relieved as hell they were both alive. *You had to. We're okay.*

She stiffened in his embrace. Her emerald eyes met his. *You mustn't touch me.*

Stop saying that. He pulled her closer. The chill clawing through his bloodstream seemed stronger now that his adrenaline was fading, and her warmth was a welcome respite. *I'm never letting you go again.* The prongs of the harp trapped between them dug into his chest. Keeping one arm firmly around her waist, he used his free hand to gently pluck the instrument from her fingertips. *How did you get this?*

From beneath her hair, a large mantis shrimp emerged on her shoulder and pumped himself up and down on his hind legs in a happy dance.

Cruz grinned. *You're one bad-ass shrimp. I owe you.*

The shrimp scurried forward and snatched the harp from his hand, then ducked back beneath Ebby's hair once more. Cruz shook his head. *You weren't kidding when you told me that harp was powerful. I'm glad you used it.*

I swore I'd never command another creature against its will. Ebby closed her eyes and laid her forehead against Cruz's shoulder, her body going limp. *Now Urokotori is dead.*

Lifting one gentle hand to her chin, Cruz tilted her face to look at him. *I hardly think killing her was against the octopus's will. I bet he's wanted to do that for ages. And he's gone, now. You freed him, didn't you? We weren't the only prisoners in this mess.*

Her trembling arms slid tentatively around his waist, the chain attaching her to the floor sliding coldly against his legs. *I suppose, yes.* She sighed, tiny bubbles escaping her lips. *I'm sorry I ran away and left you in the cave after...*

The rest of the sentence hung between them, and he felt a stirring in his groin. Her mouth was so close. So kissable. He feathered his mouth across hers, wanting her. But his chest felt tight with cold, and he could feel his fingers going numb. His dive training told him to stay on task, conserve his energy. He took her manacled hand. *Let's get you free so we can get out of here. You don't have a song to open this, do you?*

She shook her head and pulled her hand away. *Our song only works on living things. You need to swim for the surface right now before anything else happens.*

Not without you. I assume that mermaid had the key? He looked toward the corridor. *Ah, hell. Where did the octopus take her?*

There is no key. Ebby squirmed free of his embrace, pushing him toward the hatch. *You need to go back to your kind where you're safe.*

No key? He grabbed her arm again, scowling at the manacle. *She locked you up and didn't have a key?* Flipping it over, he ran his fingers along the chain. The heavy links were corroded, but still too thick and sturdy to break. What he wouldn't give for a pair of bolt cutters right now.

There may be a key somewhere on the ship. I'll send Kato to look. She lifted the shrimp off her shoulder, setting him swimming through the hatch. Then she tugged on the chain, trying to take it from him.

Anger burned inside Cruz's chest. She'd sacrificed everything for him. Now she wanted him to just abandon her? He tightened his grip. *Hell, no. You said we're mates. That means we're in this together.* He squinted around the ship's interior. *I need to search for a tool. Can you make it lighter in here?*

No. There are very few phytoplankton down here.

He stared at the minuscule drifting lights, trying to stay calm and think straight. They were like little bugs, which gave him an idea. *I used to collect fireflies in bottles as a kid.*

Releasing her hand, he swam toward the broken crates. Among the debris, several bottles remained intact. He turned to Ebby and held one up. *If we can concentrate some phytoplankton in this, we can use it like a lantern.*

He pushed at the cork, trying to dislodge it, but his hands were shaking. The chill running through his veins was infecting him with panic, despite his dive training. Turning to a crate, he swept the sediment covering the other bottles aside, hoping for one that was open. Instead, he spotted a familiar twist of metal. A corkscrew! His panic subsided. For once, luck was with him.

He began to work at the cork and then realized he was an idiot. He was holding the very tool he'd been looking for. Calf muscles threatening to cramp, he returned to Ebby's side. As he reached for her bound wrist, a bone-deep shiver rocked him. The corkscrew slid from his fingers.

Cruz? Are you all right? Ebby grabbed his shoulders. *Depths, you're freezing!*

Without warning, she put both hands to his cheeks and pressed her mouth over his. Small bubbles rose between them while her tongue played over his lips and her nipples grazed his chest. *What are you doing?* He pulled away, torn between wanting her and knowing he needed to stay on task. He ducked down to retrieve the corkscrew. *This isn't the time!*

I just refreshed your breath-spell. She pointed toward the hatch. *You need to get out of here. Now.*

Leaving you isn't an option. The breath-spell had revived him somewhat, but his heart still slammed against his ribs, trying to keep his blood flowing to his extremities. *No way in hell. Give me your hand.*

Jamming the end of the corkscrew into the lock, he began to twist.

14

The corkscrew slipped, scraping painfully into Ebby's wrist. She flinched, and he eased his grip. *Sorry. It's so dark down here.*

He rubbed his thumb over the scratch, then placed the corkscrew back into the lock. She could feel the cold taking a toll on his mind. Sapping his strength. *Cruz, go find land before you become too cold to swim. You can come back later and free me.*

He kept working. *Finding this location again would be impossible. I don't have mermaid magic to traipse around the ocean like it was my backyard. I'm lucky to have found you as it is.*

She had the feeling he meant more than simply finding the shipwreck. The determined set of his shoulders as he returned to his work made her tail fin grow weak.

Besides, I left someone once before. Turmoil filled his thoughts. *I won't do it again.*

Who did you leave?

Cruz's memories coalesced around a human contraption, and Ebby understood immediately it was something land dwellers used much like the boats they used atop the water. *My mother rolled our car into a ravine when I was seven. It was raining out, and dark. I couldn't get her seatbelt loose. Blood was everywhere. I didn't realize I'd lost my hearing, and she kept pointing out the smashed-in window. So I climbed out of the ravine to find help.* His heartbeat thudded like sonar through the dim water. For a few moments, he said nothing, continuing his work on the manacle. *Rescuers didn't locate her for two more days. She died waiting for me.*

Ebby's heart ached. Although her own mother had been cold and heartless, her father would've done anything to keep her safe. He'd even sent her away that fateful day in the Deeps when the mermaids found them. If it hadn't been for Uncle Zantu and Aunt Brianna, both she and Da would've died.

She reached up to place a palm against Cruz's cold, stubbled cheek. *You were a child. What else could you have done? Stay there and die with her? She wouldn't have wanted that.*

His throat bobbed, and he pressed one hand over hers, sandwiching her palm against him. *I won't lose another person I care about.*

Her insides fluttered. Care. That's what true mates did. She'd never thought of the bond as anything but a shackle, but it wasn't a shackle. It was a strength. The bond didn't divide her; having a devoted partner doubled her. Cruz was her mate. A loyal, caring, smart, and stupidly determined forever-mate. The other mermaids, in their quest for sexual conquest, had no idea what they were missing.

She slid closer to him, circling her hand behind his neck, and kissed him. *I love you, Cruz.*

His heartbeat quickened. Angling his head, he kissed her back, lips solid against hers. She opened her mouth, and his tongue plunged inside, his chest and thighs aligned against her body. *I love you, too.* His hand left her manacled wrist to cup her jaw, fingertips threading into her hair. His other hand feathered up her arm to her shoulder blade, pulling her tighter against his chest, kiss becoming hungrier. *You're so warm. Is it strange that I want you? Now?*

No. I want you, too. Ebby walled off her thought that this might be the last time they could be together. Arching into him, heat pooled in her middle at the feel of his erection throbbing between them. She wanted him more than she'd ever wanted anything in her entire life. All of him. No more hesitation or fear. She slid her manacled hand between them and gripped his thick shaft at the base and stroked upward slowly before angling it toward the mouth of her entrance.

He moaned into her mouth. *God, you feel so good.*

She slid forward an inch, reveling in the feel of her mate teasing her opening. His mouth left hers to trail over her collarbone then down to pull one of her nipples into his mouth. He sucked hard, drawing a cry from her that made the weak phytoplankton flicker. *Neptune*, she'd never known her body could feel this way. His tongue stroked her sensitized breast rhythmically, causing her breathing to become shallower until she was panting. Trailing biting kisses, he moved to her other nipple, gripping the back of her neck.

She wriggled against him, wanting it all. Wanting to be filled. He sucked hard at her nipple then thrust forward, burying himself inside her. She gasped, her hands on his ribcage as the chain clinked along the floorboards. His big hands pulled her hard against him, bodies meeting at every point with a heat that seemed to raise the water temperature ten degrees.

Once more his lips returned to hers, his tongue plunging into her mouth. His cock was thick and hard and she took all of him. He pulled out of her, then thrust in again. In and out, faster and faster. He was no longer cold, but searing hot. His length burned her with pleasure, with lust, his own desire matching hers as they pounded together, sending the phytoplankton into swirling patterns of brightness through the ship.

But her awareness of their surroundings barely registered as Cruz slammed into her, pounding her clit in a rhythm that wound her tighter and tighter until she was sure she couldn't take anymore. The pressure in her middle intensified, and she moaned, swept helplessly into a current of passion. She threw back her head. *Cruz, oh, depths, Cruz!*

Sensing her imminent climax, he gripped her hips and buried himself deeper, grinding hard.

Pressure changed to tingling, spreading upward from deep inside her until she exploded. Stars filled her vision, and she clutched his shoulders like a drowning woman as her warmth pulsed around him.

Cruz shuddered, a feral sound in his throat. His hips jerked, shooting throbbing jets of heat deep into her core. Moving slower, smoother, he slid in and out as his release pulsed in rhythm with hers.

Ebby relaxed, sated like she'd never been before. His lips grazed her shoulder, the base of her neck, her jawline, her lips. He tucked an errant strand of her hair behind her ear. *Well, that warmed me up.*

She smiled, her eyes fighting to stay open. *Me, too.*

Wrapping both hands around his waist to pull him close caused the chain to tangle around his leg. Reality crashed down around her. She was chained to a ship at the bottom of the ocean with a mate who was going to freeze to death or starve.

He seemed brought back to reality by the sensation, as well, reaching down to disengage himself from the links.

Much as I'd love to curl up and nap with you, I think we should get you free now.

The deep pools of his eyes were filled with such devotion, she wanted to cry. He was as stubborn as a sea otter determined to open an oyster, and no matter what she said to him, he'd stick by her until they died.

He ducked down to retrieve the corkscrew that had fallen loose during their lovemaking, and she ruefully admired his broad back, muscles rippling as he moved through the water toward the bottle that had rolled away. She would never see him at her da's nest, tidying the sponge bed, tending the seaweed garden, sunlight dancing over his skin.

Then she realized the phytoplankton surrounding him were brighter than they had been earlier, glowing like a halo. Not only around Cruz but also herself.

Holding her free hand near the lock, she illuminated the mechanism. Cruz returned to hand her the dimly glowing bottle and his mouth dropped open. *I thought you said they couldn't get any brighter.*

She shrugged, as confused as he was. *Our lovemaking must've rejuvenated them, somehow.*

He shook his head and began working on the lock. *I'll never understand mermaid magic.*

She laughed, holding still as his long deft fingers gently inserted the coiled metal into the small opening. *I think we just warmed them up is all.*

Whatever did it, I'm grateful. Face close to the metal, he rocked the corkscrew, twisting the tool back and forth.

She watched, bottom lip caught between her teeth. Having light was all well and good, but she could already feel the water cooling. Eventually, they'd be back to where they'd started. Cruz smacked the butt of his hand against the base of the corkscrew and the lock popped open. The manacle fell away, each link of the chain clunking to the floor.

You did it! Elated, Ebby put both hands on his cheeks and planted a sound kiss on his lips.

He grinned against her mouth and grabbed her hips, sweeping her into a celebratory spin. *Let's get out of here.*

She didn't need any urging. Taking his hand, she led them out of the ship's hold and toward the distant, glowing light of the sun.

15

*C*ruz kicked alongside Ebby, trying to keep up with the effortless swish of her tail. Now that he was free of the cave, the ship, and the other mermaids, he looked around the ocean with a new appreciation. To their left, a vast school of big-eyed scad darkened the water, creating cloud shapes as they evaded a smaller school of boxy-shaped jackfish. Below, a pair of gray-green dragon wrasse flipped pebbles among swaying eelgrass, taking turns eating any dislodged prey. As Ebby led him out of the deep water to the warmer currents among the coral and kelp, several orange striped butterfly fish peeked from beneath plate-shaped coral on the lower reef.

Where're we going? he asked

Ebby pulled him around the antler-like prongs of a coral and began weaving between the golden kelp fronds. *I'm taking you to my da's nest.*

He hadn't thought of mermaids having parents, and the thought of meeting her father felt strange. *I'm going to meet your dad?*

A surge of sorrow and regret filled their connection, strong enough to make him wince. *No,* she said. *He's gone.*

Cruz longed to pause and take her into his arms, but she only swam faster. *What happened to him?*

He's probably dead now. She used her free hand to push aside a thick stand of kelp and pulled them into a clearing. The oval-shaped area had a ceiling of thatched kelp fronds and the floor had been set up like a small cottage under the sea.

Dead? Cruz sized-up an antique brass headboard abutting an overflow of sea sponges arranged into a multicolored mattress. Sediment covered most surfaces, but a spot on the bed appeared to have been recently disturbed. *You don't know?*

He left when I became a mermaid. Ebby released his hand and moved to a flat stone in the center surrounded by waterlogged barrels. Taking a seat on one, she curled her tail gracefully at the barrel's base.

Her pet shrimp, Kato, had joined them as they left the ship, and now launched off her shoulder, carrying the harp to a small alcove. He promptly excavated a hole and buried the instrument. Then he began sweeping clouds of sediment from the floor with rapid movements of his tail, exposing a mosaic of shells and multi-colored stones.

Cruz moved to the barrel next to Ebby, glad to be resting after everything that had happened. *Became a mermaid?* A mirror at her back reflected her smooth back and gently rounded hips, hair floating wild and sexy about her head. He could almost imagine her with legs. *Were you human before?*

Ebby chuckled. *I forget you humans don't get to choose. Merchildren are genderless until they reach puberty.*

His gaze slid down to her breasts. *It's a little difficult to imagine you as anything other than female.* To his satisfaction, her nipples visibly tightened. Hunger for her drove heat to his groin. But her mind was full of sadness, and he wanted their next lovemaking to be full of joy, not sorrow or regret. *Why did your choice of gender make your dad leave?*

She chewed her lip, gaze sliding down to the tabletop. *He didn't trust being around me. Mermaids are dangerous.*

Indignation burned in his heart. *But he was your father.*

Doesn't matter. She reached out and swept sediment off the surface in front of her, exposing the pitted stone beneath. *Mermaids are violent, possessive, and can't be trusted, not even with their family.*

She'd mentioned before that mermaids were bad. That all they wanted to do was play, and most of their entertainment was some form of torture. But Ebby was a mermaid, and that wasn't her at all. *If they're so bad, why did you choose to be female?*

A wistful smile swept over her features. *As a child, I always assumed I'd choose male. I used to play nest building, and I helped with the baby before...* She swallowed visibly. *The baby died. But when the time came, the choice was clear. I didn't want to end up like my da.*

What do you mean? There was so much about Ebby he didn't understand, and the more he learned, the more he wanted to know.

Her free hand clenched into a fist on the table. *I never wanted to be a slave to the mate bond.*

His throat tightened. Strange as it was, he was delighted with this bond that allowed him to share himself with another person. On land, he could never have something like this, not even with a wife. A mate who could hear him was so much better, and he could easily envision himself living beneath the waves with Ebby for eternity. He'd never considered that perhaps Ebby didn't want to be attached to him. He released her and folded his hands in his lap.

If you don't want to be attached to me, you can take me back to land. I'll be all right. That was a complete lie, but he'd find no joy in a life with someone who didn't want him.

No! She reached toward him, then hesitated, her delicate brows furrowed. *Unless you don't want to stay with me? I won't force you.*

Cruz melted, relief flooding him. He lifted her, carrying her toward the bed. *I'd like nothing better than to spend the rest of my life with you.*

She closed her eyes and leaned against his chest. He settled her against the soft sponge mattress and lay down next to her, cocooning her in his arms. The next thing he knew, darkness had fallen. Ebby lay slumbering in his arms, warm and soft. He'd never felt so at home, like he'd finally found where he belonged, right here in her embrace.

She must've sensed he'd woken because she turned to face him. *I promise I will never do to you what my mother did to Da.*

Have you been awake thinking this whole time? He pulled her closer against his chest.

I dozed. I just want you to know you are safe with me.

What did your mother do? Were your she and father mated like us?

Oh, no. A harsh laugh shook Ebby's chest. *My father adored my mother. He couldn't help it. But she didn't return his love. Every time she left us, she took a little piece of him with her until he was a mere husk of a man. I* was glad when she finally died because it meant Da was free. She sighed heavily. *Only, he wasn't. Not really.*

Humans call it depression.

She seemed to shrink in his arms. *When I became female, it broke him for good.*

He put a hand on the soft skin of her cheek. *You cannot blame yourself for the way someone else feels.*

One of her fingers traced over his lips, sending a shiver through him. *Not even you?*

He gently bit her fingertip, holding it between his teeth. *Depends on what kind of feel we're talking about.*

She wriggled slightly, and his cock surged to attention. *How about that kind of feel?*

Splaying his hand on the small of her back, he ran it up her spine until it tangled in her hair. Gently, he tugged her head back and to the side, leaning forward to brush his lips against her throat. Her breasts were soft against his chest, her skin silky on his mouth.

He dragged his free hand up her ribs and cupped her breast. Her chest heaved in an excited breath and her nipple tightened. Lifting himself on one arm, he rolled her back against the sponges. He couldn't see her in the dark, but he could feel her desire meeting his through their mental connection, urging him on.

He rubbed the smooth skin over her hips and up to the transition of her belly, over her breasts, stroking her cheek. With gentle, feathering kisses, he worshipped her, adored her, covering every inch of her skin before he slid one hand down her taut belly to her sex. Her folds were slick and waiting, and she arched upward into his touch. Without hesitation, he buried his middle finger inside her.

You're so perfect, he said as he slowly fingered her.

She rolled her hips against his touch. He inserted a second finger, his thighs straddling her. Her inner walls pulsed around him, quivering with every stroke against her innermost ridges. She bucked and writhed, reaching for him with both hands and pulling him down atop her. Her mouth met his, soft and yielding, one hand cupping the back of his head. The tips of their tongues met, sending a blaze of desire up his spine.

Never breaking the kiss, he reached down between them, positioning himself at her entrance. She rocked against his dick and he groaned mindlessly. In one swift thrust, he buried himself inside her. She rolled against him again and he kissed her harder, one hand cupping her cheek as he rode her. She felt so good wrapped around him, so tight and hot. A perfect fit. A perfect mate.

She bucked up to match his rhythm, their bodies moving together, and he buried his face against her neck, crushing her body to his, rolling his hips faster. Her skin tasted dewy and musky, driving him wild as he slid in and out of her. The pressure inside him built with every stroke, and he could feel within her mind that she was also on the edge of ecstasy, panting his name with every thrust.

One hand bracing her hips, he ground into her, gritting his teeth against his orgasm. He pulled back, hovering at the edge of her entrance. *Come for me*, he growled and slammed back inside her.

She let out a cry and arched upward, rocking with the first pulse of her orgasm. He clutched her tighter as the water buoyed them upward, continuing his thrusting until he was sure he'd pulled every last response from her body. With a shudder and a groan of his own, he allowed her aftershocks to milk him into oblivion.

16

The morning song of a batfish outside the nest woke Ebby. She stretched and opened her eyes. Cruz slept soundly beside her on the sponge bed, one arm pillowing her head, the other wrapped loosely over her hip. Quietly, she tried to sit. His arm around her hip tightened and pulled her backward against him.

Not so fast. His voice in her head was adorably groggy. *Where's my morning kiss?*

She smiled and turned in the circle of his arms to place her palm on his stubbled cheek. Nibbling kisses against his lips, she said, *I'm hungry.*

Me, too. Cruz kissed her firmly and sat up. *I would offer to cook you breakfast, but I'm not sure what you have to eat around here. Or how to cook it.*

Ebby'd heard of this 'cooking' thing, but the purpose was a mystery to her. She rose from the bed, looking around for the knife Da used to keep for harvests. *I'll show you the gardens.*

Sediment had all but smothered the patch of seaweed just outside the nest, but Da had kept several plots of seaweed farther out along the reef. Handing Cruz a knife, she led him through the thatched kelp and out of the clearing to a leeward stretch of stone where the seaweed had once grown thick and lush. Her infrequent visits weren't enough to maintain the gardens, and several parrotfish had moved in, shearing the bulk of the succulent fronds.

Sending a sonic warning to chase the fish away, she escorted Cruz among the patchy growth, teaching him how to harvest, how to remove the invading sea slugs, and how to avoid the anemones hiding among the fronds. *Tending the gardens is part of keeping a nest,* she explained, then realized with giddy joy that she had a nest. A nest she wouldn't only visit occasionally, but one she would help maintain, with Cruz at her side.

Cruz sampled various bites as they filled the bowl. *I could really go for a cheeseburger right now.*

What's a cheeseburger?

Meat with melted cheese between two soft buns. He held up a frond, eyeing it critically before stuffing it into his mouth. *Kind of hard to explain, but I'm making myself hungrier thinking about it. This is like only getting the lettuce.*

You'll be too full to eat when we get back, she teased.

He wrapped an arm around her waist and held a piece to her lips. *You'd better eat, too. I have other plans than eating when we get back.*

Giggling, she accepted the bite, sucking his finger playfully.

Naughty mermaid. He grinned at her.

She wrapped both hands around his backside and gripped his hips, grinding herself against his growing erection. *Insatiable human.*

Something gold caught the light on the rise above them, and a pair of citrine-colored eyes met hers above a red sea fan. Ebby shoved Cruz behind her.

Rising from the ridge, Lutana's coral lips spread into a grin.

Fuck! Where's my knife? Cruz scrambled toward the bowl of seaweed resting between the rocks several meters away.

Ebby rose into the current, hands on her hips, and glared at the other mermaid. Lutana by herself Ebby could handle. But if she'd brought friends... "What do you want?"

Lutana cocked her head. "The currents are singing that Selachii and Urokotori are dead."

Ebby glared at Lutana in silent challenge. "I can't imagine you have a problem with that, Lutana. You'll no longer be forced to play their games."

Cruz floated up beside Ebby, knife brandished in one hand. *Found it.*

Tinkling laughter rippled the water. "Oh, he's a fierce one, isn't he?" The golden mermaid's gaze swept over Cruz. "How long do you plan on keeping him?"

Throat tight, Ebby considered her next words. There was no rule protecting a mermaid's mates, likely because mermaids had no affection for any given merman. But

Cruz was human. Didn't that make him special? Kato peeked cautiously from beneath a palm coral, giving Ebby an idea. "He's my new pet."

Lutana narrowed her eyes, lips curling into a scowl. "You are the strangest mermaid I know. The others are going to find this quite interesting."

"Others?"

"Like I said, the currents are already whispering about the open territory." Lutana shrugged and turned to go.

"What if I told you he's my mate?" Ebby blurted.

Lutana halted, then moved back to the edge of the ridge, her shrewd gaze once more raking Cruz from head to toe. "I think you're confused, sister. You're a mermaid. Not some love-sick merman."

A part of Ebby felt sorry for Lutana. The other mermaid didn't revel in cruelty like Selachii and Urokotori had, but she was still influenced by their expectations. Ebby moved forward. "We don't have to be defined by our gender or our sexuality. Only our actions."

Lutana blew out a sharp string of bubbles and crossed her arms.

Ebby moved forward a few centimeters. "It's not too late for you, Lutana. If I can find love, then so can you."

Lutana made a non-committal sound in the back of her throat, then without another word, spun and disappeared over the rise.

There will be other mermaids, won't there? Cruz's voice entered softly into her head. *Someday, one of us will get hurt.*

Briny tears stung Ebby's eyes. Her dream of having a nest with a mate and partner, a dream that had seemed so real only moments ago, had been ripped from its roots like kelp during a storm. She turned to Cruz, taking in his muscular handsomeness, from his rippled chest and strong arms to the legs he kicked gently to keep himself afloat. It would have been difficult enough to protect a merman as a mate, but a human was all but helpless beneath the waves. If only he could grow a tail like Uncle Zantu had grown legs...

A dam inside her chest opened. Was there another way? How had Uncle Zantu grown legs? There was only one way to find out. She took Cruz's hands in hers. *I have someone I want to introduce you to.*

*E*bby cautiously approached the small cove where her uncle lived. A storm was coming, and the waves crashed strongly against the shore. She struggled to resist the undertow that wanted to toss her and Cruz against the rocky bottom.

A small yacht bobbed in the surf near the point, making her pause. The beach wasn't private, but unless one had a boat, it could only be accessed by climbing over the sharp, surf-washed boulders on either side of the crescent-shaped beach. *Depths,* of course she'd choose the day someone decided to drop in for a picnic.

What is it? Cruz asked as she sent a sonic query to the nearby fish, asking how long the vessel had been here.

She pointed toward the shadow of the boat above them. *I don't know who that belongs to.*

He tilted his head and his grip on her hand tightened. *That might be my friends, looking for me.*

Gesturing to her billowing tail fin, she said, *I can't let humans see me like this.*

The current drove them toward a submerged boulder, forcing her to pull Cruz crosswise to avoid it. She backed them farther from shore and wrapped her arms around his neck, burying her head against the crook of his shoulder. She couldn't imagine life without him. But if she was bound to the sea, and he to the land, how could they make a life together?

He cupped the back of her head and pressed a kiss against her ear. *We could go find another beach.*

There're no other beaches without humans. She thought of the coastline, miles of noisy boats, people swimming, homes overlooking the water. *And I need to talk to my Uncle.* She'd told him about her uncle while they swam to the cove, and how he'd grown legs to be with his mate on land. But she was a mermaid, and that might not be possible for her.

Ebby. He craned his neck to look into her eyes. *We'll just wait until the boat leaves, okay?*

A ragged clump of feathers drifted by, the remnants of some bird fallen prey to the dangers of the ocean. Cruz wasn't safe here. He had to go back right away, whether she could join him or not. *You should go and tell your friends you're all right. I'll come in once the coast is clear.*

He gripped her tighter. *We've been through this. I won't leave you.*

She grimaced. *There's a storm coming. Staying this close to shore is dangerous. You need to go to land.*

His mouth thinned into a dissatisfied line. After a moment, he said, *Promise me you'll come to shore as soon as you can?*

She nodded. *I promise.*

Keeping them below the surface until she was certain he could power through the waves on his own, she released him to strike out in long, powerful strokes toward shore. When he reached shallower water, she bobbed in the waves with only her eyes above the surface, watching him rise out of the surf. His muscular form was even more magnificent on land, water gleaming from his golden tanned skin in the sunlight. Oh, how she loved the broad muscles of his shoulders and the defined cords of his legs.

Propelling herself back out of the cove and away from the surging waves, she rolled onto her back and stared at her tail. Could she grow legs like Uncle Zantu had? He'd told her it had something to do with the mate-bond. Without Cruz here, fear struck her that mermaids really might impervious to the mate bond. What if she'd only imagined the connection all along? Now that Cruz was on land, maybe the magic was broken.

The crashing waves could be dangerous, even for a mermaid, but she couldn't resist moving into the maze of submerged boulders along the south edge of the cove, just to be closer to Cruz. Holding herself vertically, like a razorfish in the spines of a sea urchin, she poked the top of her head above the waves. On the beach, two men conversed, but there could be other humans farther back among the trees. She dared not show herself until she was sure it was safe. How close did she have to be to talk to Cruz? *Cruz, can you hear me?*

No response.

Her fin grated along the rocky bottom and she gritted

her teeth. She couldn't get much closer without ending up bruised and bloodied. Over the roar of the waves, a child's laughter sprinkled the air.

Ebby lifted her head and shoulders above the water for a better look, praying no one saw her among the rocks.

A small figure that could only be Camilla jumped up and down on top of Ebby's favorite boulder, talking to someone in the water. Brianna? The human liked to swim, but Ebby was surprised to see her braving this kind of surf. Most likely she was trying to get Camilla to come off that rock and back to shore.

Uncle Zantu's voice echoed from the beach, barely audible over the crashing waves. "Come on, Ebby! It's fine!"

Relief so great it took her breath away swept through Ebby's chest. Cruz had done it! He'd met her uncle and now everything was going to be okay. Keeping her head above water, she pulled herself from among the boulders and allowed a curling wave to carry her forward. Her heart swelled as she recognized her uncle's silver-blue hair and Cruz's broad shoulders, both men facing the water.

Ebby! Cruz called, his faint voice infused with excitement.

Then a flash of emerald behind Camilla's rock made Ebby's heart falter. Was that a mermaid? Where was Brianna? Dread took root in Ebby's stomach. Was everyone on shore under a mermaid's spell?

A deep, familiar song pulsed through the water, a lullaby she hadn't heard in over two years. She froze, confused, as another wave broke over her, driving her against the sand.

She surfaced again as an emerald-tailed merman pulled himself onto the rock near Camilla.

"Da?" She couldn't breathe, couldn't move. Da was alive! Alive and here! "I thought you'd died!"

Her father's wary eyes met hers before glancing over his shoulder toward the beach. "You're sure she's no danger?"

Camilla threw her arms around the merman's neck. "Stop worrying, Uncle Rubac. Ebby would never hurt anyone."

The elation in Ebby's heart soured. He was still terrified. Still believed she would rip him apart just for fun.

Cruz's soothing voice came to her. *He doesn't know any better. Not yet.*

Ebby pulled herself onto another boulder several meters away from him, hands gripping its barnacled surface as another wave tried to push her over. Cruz was right. She needed to move slowly, even though she yearned to race to her father, to hug him like Camilla was now. But she understood his fear.

He remained silent, gaze drifting over her apricot tail. He looked the same as she remembered, emerald tail just as bright, jewelry gleaming from every limb and piercing. What should she say to him? Her voice wobbled in her throat as she fought back tears. "Hi, Da."

Camilla let go of Rubac's neck and stood to face Ebby again, her pudgy belly pink from the cold water. She wore a frilly two-piece bathing suit that made her hips look like a jellyfish. "He has a new mate named Madison! She brought me candy. Come on! I bet she'll give you some, too!"

A second mate? Ebby hadn't thought that was possible. "You have another mate?"

Da rubbed a hand through his hair, brow furrowed. "I don't know what to call her, but I love her."

Ebby looked toward shore. Cruz had moved into the waves, wobbling with each shove of water against his legs. If Da had a mate, he should have legs, right? Maybe the magic was special only for Uncle Zantu...

Shaking her head, she shoved the thought away. By Neptune, she was going to grow legs if she had to cut herself in half to do it. She pushed herself off the rock toward shore. "I have a mate, too."

Cruz raised both arms toward her. *Come to me, Eb—ah, hell!* A wave swept his feet out from under him.

Ebby plunged forward, grabbing him before the wave could roll him into the undertow. Next thing she knew, rocks were digging into her back and Cruz lay on top of her as the wave departed, leaving them exposed on land.

He looked into her eyes, gaze reflecting love as surely as moonlight reflected off a calm sea. Pushing up onto his hands, he rocked back on his heels. His eyes moved down her torso and came to rest somewhere below her belly, and a slow grin spread across his lips.

She followed his gaze to a flattened triangle of hair just below her belly button and bolted upright. Her apricot tail had been replaced by long, pale thighs, knees and shins, and feet with ten perfect pink toes covered in sand. "I did it!" She looked up into his eyes. "I really did it!"

Camilla raced up, holding up a pink and purple towel. "Want to use my towel?"

Ebby took it, knowing humans had an aversion to nakedness, and wrapped it around herself. She'd never been self-conscious as a mermaid, but this new body was too fresh, too new for her to feel comfortable in it yet, anyway. "Thank you, Camilla."

Another wave came crashing toward them, and Cruz slipped his arms beneath her shoulders and knees, carrying her as easily as she'd transported him through the water.

"C'mon Ebby." The little girl grabbed her hand. "Let's ask Madison for more candy!"

"Hold on, little nibbler." Uncle Zantu swept in and lifted his daughter to his shoulders. "Ebby needs some time to adjust and maybe talk to her da before we make her race up the hill."

The little girl started to complain, but Ebby smiled at her cousin and promised, "I'll be up soon, okay?"

"Hurry, please." Then Camilla squealed in glee as Zantu started jogging up the path.

Cruz carried her across the sand toward her father. He stopped at the edge of the crashing surf and lowered Ebby's feet to the sand. *You want me to leave you alone?*

No! She took his hand, glancing up into his face. *Depths, you're tall!*

He chuckled out loud. *No more fins to make you seem big.*

Or scary, she thought as she turned back to the surf where Da waited, head and shoulders above water. Signing and speaking at the same time, she said, "Da, I'd like you to meet my mate, Cruz. Cruz, this is my father, Rubac."

Da couldn't seem to drag his gaze from her legs.

Cruz signed, "Happy to meet you, sir."

"He says happy to meet you," Ebby translated.

Da blinked, finally seeming to notice Cruz. A slow smile spread over his face. "Your mate. He has a good aura. Strong." His eyes met hers. "As do you, my daughter."

Ebby's heart developed a pang she wasn't sure how to interpret. "Da, are... are you still afraid of me?"

Da shook his head and moved toward shore until his tail was fully exposed and gleaming in the frothing water. "Come give me a hug."

Stumbling forward in the wet sand, Ebby dropped to her knees and threw her arms around his neck, a sob sticking in her throat. "I missed you so much."

His arms wrapped around her shoulders, one hand patting her gently. "When you decided to become female, I thought you'd never be the same. I thought you'd turn into a monster. I was wrong. I'm sorry." He squeezed her tighter. "And I'm proud of you."

"I love you, Da," Ebby choked out, squeezing her father hard.

"I love you, too, Ebby." A wave surged over them, nearly pulling the towel free, and she released her hug to keep it in place.

Da drifted back into the water, but he didn't stray far.

As she rose to her feet, Cruz stepped forward and put an arm around her to steady her. *Everything good now?*

Leaning against him, she wiggled her toes in the damp sand, watching her father's emerald tail. *Everything's amazing.*

From the water, Da called out, "Now go up and introduce yourself to Madison. Then tell her to come down here. I think it's time we had a proper family reunion."

*E*bby straddled Cruz where he lay on the beach blanket, still amazed by the feel of him between her thighs, and looked out over the waves. The wind coming off the water had picked up, kicking sand over the rocks, while the sunset painted the sky vanilla yellow. Music drifted down from the cottage up the hill, partygoers having abandoned the beach in favor of pizza and party games.

Ebby took in a long, slow breath of salty air, thinking of the cake she'd baked for Camilla's birthday. Since coming on shore, Ebby'd developed quite a taste for human foods, especially chocolate, and spent much of her time in the kitchen experimenting with different flavors. Her butterscotch seaweed hadn't been much of a hit, but her chocolate dulse-cake was good enough that Camilla'd requested it for her party.

"What are you thinking?" Cruz signed.

They'd developed some basic rules about delving into each other's minds in the months they'd been on land, not to mention the courtesy of allowing the people around them to participate in their conversations. Zantu and Brianna still needed Ebby to translate most things, but Camilla was already fluent. She might not have a tail, but it seemed she'd inherited a mermaid's ability to pick up languages as easily as she collected seashells.

Since they were alone, Ebby opened her thoughts to her mate. She wasn't exactly sure how to approach the subject she really wanted to talk about. *I could sure go for some chocolate right now.*

He laughed and ran a light finger down her spine. *Shall we go see if Camilla has left us any cake?* His hand slipped into the waistband of her swimsuit to cup her ass. *Or do you want to stay here?*

She giggled, clenching her buttocks, still unused to the new sensations of being human. Or at least, of having a human shape. She would always be a mermaid. *I'm not a fan of sand in my crevices. But I'd really like some cake.*

He wiggled his fingers, sand already grating her skin, and she squealed, trying to squirm away. He held her firmly, flipping her onto her back. A giggle drew her attention and Ebby tapped Cruz's chest. *We have company.*

Cruz rolled away while Ebby straightened her swim top. At the bottom of the path, Camilla's pixie face grinned at them from behind a tree.

Ebby rose, hands on her hips. "Camilla, spying is rude."

Camilla waited until Cruz faced her, then signed, "Mommy says to bring you up before we light the candles."

"All right, little nibbler." Cruz used the family's name for the child, and Ebby's heart felt like it might burst. He'd make a great father. "We're right behind you."

As he shook out the blanket, Ebby decided to approach her issue in a more straightforward manner. She'd never discussed children with Cruz and was still uncertain about her abilities as a mother, but she'd already thrown aside her misconception about a mermaid's heart being incapable of loving a mate. Why not a child? *Ever think you might want one of those?*

One of what? He rolled the blanket around their water bottles and tucked it under one arm.

Ebby donned her flip flops, her heart in her throat. *A little nibbler.*

Cruz raised an eyebrow at her. *I'd love nothing more. Is there something you want to tell me?*

Ebby'd been waiting for the right moment for two days now, ever since Brianna had helped her use the home pregnancy test. She'd cried over the little plus sign on the stick, fearful of the future, of her skills and responsibilities. Brianna had held her, promising to be there every step of the way, and at that moment, Ebby'd decided to go ahead and try. Perhaps she'd have a little boy like Cruz, with dark hair and hazel eyes and a smile that melted her heart.

She bit her lip and looked at her mate through her lashes. *I hear if it's a girl, I'll crave chocolate and pickles.*

Cruz's eyes widened then he dropped the blanket and put both hands on her shoulders. *I'm going to be a father?*

She nodded.

He let out a yell and swept her into his arms. *Have I told you I love you today?*

Ebby wrapped both legs around his waist, letting his joy sweep over her. She could do this. With the love of her mate, she could do anything. *Better tell me again just to be sure.*

I love you. He kissed her slowly, lingering over her mouth with soft, slow strokes of his tongue.

She pulled him more tightly against her. *I love you, too.*

*D*ear Reader,

Thank you for reading Ebby's story. I hope you liked my take on mermaid mythology! Are you craving more sweet and steamy magical romance? Check out my newest series, Alaska Alphas. Book one starts with an outcast shifter who wanders the Alaskan wilderness alone—until he saves a witch's life. Can their forbidden love find a happily ever after?

Keep reading for a sneak peek!

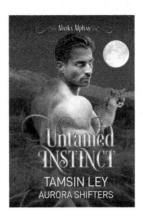

P.S. Do you want to know what happened to Kato? Join my VIP Club and get a bonus epilogue that didn't quite fit in this book but should answer a few more questions for you

SIGN UP HERE:
https://bookhip.com/SNLNWR

UNTAMED INSTINCT

SNEAK PEEK

*A*drian crouched among the cottonwood leaves, claws digging into the bark as he surveyed the dead moose in the clearing below. He'd been waiting here in his mountain lion form for several hours and was eager to move on, but had to be certain the carcass had been deserted before he drew closer to investigate. He'd received numerous reports of abandoned animal kills over the last few weeks, and his supervisor at the ranger station wanted whoever—or whatever—was doing the poaching to be tracked down.

Scattered throughout the Wrangell-St. Elias Park, the previous sites had been old before Adrian reached them, the evidence around the carcasses obscured by smaller predators and decay. This site seemed fresher, the stench of rot less intense, although flies swarmed over the bull's hide and stubby, velvet-covered antlers. If the killer was human, they weren't out for trophies. And they definitely weren't doing it for meat. Someone or something was killing for fun, and they were slowly moving closer to human-occupied lands.

Adrian's tail twitched angrily, and he let out a grunt of resignation before dropping nimbly to the ground. The scent of rotting flesh grew stronger as he approached, and flies rose in a cloud, exposing gashes writhing with fresh maggots.

He circled the moose, estimating it had been dead slightly longer than twenty-four hours. Clawed paw prints, almost twice the size of his own, scarred the earth around the kill. He lowered his muzzle and sniffed, tail lashing. The familiar musk of a grizzly filled his nose. *Shifter grizzly.* He released a hiss of displeasure. The last thing the shifter community wanted was a rogue member drawing attention to the national park. Randall, Adrian's tough-as-nails wolf supervisor, would not like this.

Fuck, Adrian didn't like it either. Mountain lions weren't unheard of in Alaska, but rare enough to cause a ruckus among humans if sighted. The vast wilds of the park were his refuge—his *territory* in the mind of his mountain lion. The local bear shifters would want to take care of a rogue grizzly themselves.

Adrian exposed his canines and turned away, prowling through the trees toward his ranger cabin to call his supervisor.

Just out of sight of his cabin, he shifted and retrieved the uniform he kept in a hollow tree, shrugging into his clothing before emerging into the clearing. His cabin was a small log building nestled next to one of the many rock faces jutting from the mountain, roof covered in thick moss and a small porch screened in from mosquitoes. One of the more popular trailheads started nearby, and a small message board fluttered with notices campers left to each other at the end of his overgrown driveway.

Inside the two-room cabin, a few small windows shed dusky light over the sparse furnishings. Passing the small front area with a table, a propane fridge, a wood stove, and an old sofa, he moved to the bedroom where a king-sized bed took up almost every inch of space. He retrieved his cell phone from the nightstand and moved to the corner of the front room where he got the best reception. He kept an old ham radio in the shed for when the notoriously spotty cell service didn't work, but he couldn't talk to Randall about shifter business over the radio. Thankfully, the phone showed two bars today. He dialed the main ranger office.

"This is HQ," a woman's nasal voice answered.

"Cherry, it's Adrian. I need to talk to Randall."

"Oh, hi, handsome!" Her voice brightened. "We haven't heard from you in a while. How've you been?"

Adrian bared his teeth and reminded himself to be polite; Cherry was human. "Doing fine."

He hated social niceties, which was why he'd become a ranger in the first place. This remote location suited him well, and he only ventured into town when he needed supplies. Most of his duties allowed him to patrol the trails alone, talking to the occasional hiker and reporting any problems. Several times a year he had to oversee search and rescue operations when a hiker got lost, but more often than not, he found the missing person before a full team even arrived.

"You doing okay on handouts?" Cherry chirped back.

He glanced toward the door where a stack of papers had gathered a layer of dust. He was supposed to pass them out to tourists, but since he avoided people, he used very few. "All good. I just need to talk to Randall."

"You betcha."

The phone clicked. A few heartbeats later, the supervisor's voice came on the line. "Adrian, what's up?"

"I've got a lead on the poacher. I found a spike-fork moose abandoned yesterday, and there's fresh grizzly sign all over the place. Smells like a shifter."

"Shit. Don't tell me the infection's moved to our territory."

"What infection?"

"Rogues." The sound of fingernails against beard stubble scratched over the phone line. "Two rogue wolves and a moose were put down in Anchorage over the winter, then a black bear outside Valdez this spring. No rhyme or reason to why. Council sent out a memo a while back. Don't you read your emails, Adrian?"

Adrian glanced at the dust-covered laptop under the nightstand. "Not like I have wifi out here, Randall. I'll catch up next time I go into town."

Randall made a frustrated noise over the phone. "Well, if a shifter's behind these abandoned kills, it's likely a rogue. File your report then go handle it ASAP."

"Me? Isn't this Den business?" Although the Council oversaw shifter law, local shifter groups liked to take care of their own business.

"Not this time. A travel blogger already posted about the kills. We need to get ahead of the news before it goes viral. Take your rifle."

"I'm a ranger, not a SWAT team, Randall."

"This is your territory. I need you to handle it. There could be hikers in danger."

"Fuck." Adrian grimaced. "What if he shifts before he dies?" It was one thing for a ranger to take down a dangerous bear. Quite another if a human body showed up killed by a ranger's bullet. And in a face-to-face fight, a mountain lion couldn't stand up to a full-grown grizzly, especially a shifter gone rogue.

"Make your first shot count."

"I hate this shit." Hanging up, Adrian pocketed his phone and grabbed his rifle before heading back outside. He'd file a report when he got back. Best to get on the trail while it was still relatively warm.

He started up his ATV, its disused engine letting out a disgusting belch of smoke. The damn thing cut off his ability to hear or smell anything, which made his mountain lion bristle in discomfort. *I know, me too.* But he couldn't carry his rifle while in feline form.

Stowing the weapon in the mounted case on the front of the ATV, he rolled out of the cabin's clearing toward the trailhead parking lot.

CHAPTER TWO

Darcy stopped her Subaru and eyed the overgrown path. According to Google, this dirt road should lead to a trailhead parking lot, but it looked like if she drove any farther, she might end up "parked" more permanently. Her all-wheel drive had managed the old, rutted road, but the path was getting narrower, with branches rubbing her door panels. *Did I take a wrong turn?*

She glanced in her rearview mirror. There had been a space wide enough to turn around a short way back. Putting the car in reverse, she carefully maneuvered through the brush, backing into a flat area that looked like it would make a nice campsite.

The overcast sky filtered dimly through the thick canopy of trees, and she hadn't seen a soul since turning into what had started out as a fairly decent dirt road. She rolled down her window and breathed in the verdant forest air. *This looks like as good a place to start as any.*

Her interview with the coven was the day after tomorrow, and she'd come in search of herbs to make an eloquence potion. This would be her last-ditch effort to overcome the stutter that ruined every spell she tried to cast. Poor Aunt Willow still had a patch of white hair behind one ear from one of her lessons. Darcy'd tried to buy an eloquence potion from the local apothecary shop, but it turned out it only worked for the person who made it, and the effects would not be permanent. But she didn't need to be *good* at incantations, only steady enough to pass the coven's apprenticeship test.

Cutting the engine, she reached over to the passenger seat to retrieve her copy of *Wild Edible and Medicinal Plants of the Pacific Northwest*. She was more familiar

A MERMAID'S HEART

with gardens than wilderness, but her mom had sent her to summer camp every year of her childhood, and the forest didn't daunt her.

Tapping her phone, she opened her GPS app and pinned her current location so she could find her way back, then tucked it and the book into a reusable grocery bag alongside a small trowel, a pair of purple and yellow gardening gloves, and a compact rain poncho. She looked around as she stepped out of the car, taking in a circle of stones around an overgrown fire pit. The mossy log seats around it obviously hadn't been disturbed in quite a while, and knee-high saplings and brush filled the clearing.

Locking the car even though she doubted she needed to, she headed toward what looked like a trail on the uphill side of the clearing. According to her book, wild rhodiola rosea grew on rocky slopes at high altitudes.

She set off between the trees, scanning the surrounding plants for signs of fleshy rhodiola leaves. A thick layer of dry leaves and twigs crunched under her feet, birds sang overhead, and in the distance a woodpecker tatted out a rhythm. She let out a contented sigh, running her fingertips over the smooth gray trunk of a quaking aspen as she passed.

A scraggly thicket of salmonberries crowded the trail, and she sampled a few, letting the sweet juice coat her tongue. A mosquito buzzed her ear, and she reached into her bag for her homemade insect repellant. She wasn't yet much good at magical potions, but she had a decent grasp of essential oils, and her minty-citrus concoction not only worked, it smelled good. After dousing herself, she tucked the small spray bottle away and continued on.

The path grew steeper, making her calves burn as she climbed until she reached a sharp turn. To her right, the trail paralleled the top of a rocky ridge, but about fifteen feet below, she spotted a clump of rosette shaped leaves. *Rhodiola?* She stepped toward the edge to get a better look.

The ground beneath her feet collapsed. Too startled to even scream, she bumped and slithered helplessly down the incline on her backside, coming to a stop among a rain of pebbles and dust.

More stunned than hurt, she sat up and pushed her strawberry blonde hair out of her face before struggling to her feet. Other than a few scrapes and a racing heartbeat, she wasn't hurt, thank the Goddess. Next to her, scaly rosettes of rhodiola crouched staunchly among the rocks. Amidst the dust, her minty-citrus scented insect repellant had become cloying. She pulled the crushed bottle from her bag and wrinkled her nose. Oily residue covered everything inside. She wiped her phone and the book on the leg of her jeans. At least she'd be insect-free for a while.

Along the cliff face behind her, a scoured swath of dirt and stone showed her path down the steep incline. It was a wonder she wasn't seriously injured. She peered both directions along the wall. Not one spot looked possible to climb.

"Fuck," she muttered. Her stutter never affected her curse words.

She turned back to the rhodiola. *Might as well make the most of the situation before I try to climb back up.* She pulled out her book to make sure the photos matched, then put on her gardening gloves and shoved a clump aside to get at the root. The plant seemed to grow directly from a crack in one of the large stones. If she could've used store-bought herbs, she would've, but for this potion, the rhodiola root had to be freshly gathered within seventy-two hours after a full moon.

Jabbing the pointed end of her trowel into the crack, she tried to pry it apart, but the tool scraped uselessly against the stone. She tried several angles, but the ground refused to give up its hold on the plant. Standing upright, she glared toward the overcast sky in frustration.

As if the heavens were laughing at her, a fat raindrop hit her square on the forehead. *Great.*

She wiped at the moisture with the back of one wrist, moving on to another nearby plant. All she succeeded in doing was breaking a fingernail down to the quick and snapping a few stems off at ground level. "I need these damn roots."

How could this be so hard? Her trowel didn't give her enough leverage against the rocks. She would have to come back with a full-sized shovel and try again. At least she knew where the rhodiola was now.

Stuffing her trowel and gloves back into her bag, she pulled out her phone to mark the spot on her app.

No reception.

She held the phone overhead and paced a few feet in either direction, waiting for a signal. The app refused to come up. Maybe the rock wall was blocking her. *God, what a day.*

Well, as long as she didn't stray from the wall, she wouldn't end up walking in circles. Eventually, she'd get reception again. Or at least find a relatively easy spot to climb and get back to the trail.

Phone in hand, she began walking along the base of the cliff.

CHAPTER THREE

Adrian stopped his ATV next to a blue Subaru Forester and cut the engine. What was a car doing so far off the road? He dismounted and circled the vehicle. Judging by the tire tracks, it'd only been here a few hours. A single set of footprints—a woman's, he'd guess by the size— headed straight toward a game trail that led to the moose kill site. He'd need to hurry if he wanted to catch her before she reached it.

He shouldered his rifle and started off, yearning for the ease of his mountain lion form. Where the trail veered to follow a ridge, a swath of fresh dirt marred the edge. Cautious of an undercut, he edged closer and peered over the drop-off. That landslide was definitely not the product of a controlled descent, but he didn't see a body. He called out, "Hello, anyone down there?"

Only wind rustling the leaves responded.

Sniffing the breeze, he tried to detect if the woman was still nearby. A delicious odor wafted toward him, masking all other scents and making his inner feline wriggle. *Catnip?* How strange.

Since the footprints ended here, he would have to investigate. He clambered down using his hands and feet. Descending as a mountain lion would've been easier, but approaching a frightened hiker as a predator was never a good idea, let alone one as rare as a mountain lion.

At the bottom, the strong essence of catnip made his feline instincts claw for attention. Reigning in his desire to shed his clothing and roll around on his back, he found the scuff marks of the woman's shoes and followed her trail.

Loose sand and random boulders made walking difficult, but the trail of catnip led him forward even when the footprints weren't clear. At a large tree, several limbs had been freshly broken, as if the woman had tried to climb up.

The scent of catnip was stronger here, as well as the delicious scent of female. Floral with a hint of sweet black tea, it reminded him of his early days with his mother, before his mountain lion had emerged, before the pack rejected him. A mountain lion didn't belong among wolves. He was what they called a "sport," an offspring with unexpected traits inherited from a long-ago ancestor.

The female scent in the area made his uniform trousers feel uncomfortably tight. *Mate*, his mountain lion purred. Adrian's balls agreed, but his head knew better. The catnip had to be messing with his senses. While he appreciated human females, he'd never met one who made him want to claim her. He was thinking about claiming this one sight-unseen.

And the heady scent was powerful, driving him forward even more than his duty to protect a hiker.

Ahead, another tree had four deep gouges staining the papery white trunk with lines of sap. *Claws.* This was a fresh bear marking. Adrian sniffed the air, senses muddied by warm female and dizzying catnip. The grizzly shifter had been here. Had made this mark. But something was off about the scent, a cloying, ashy odor that made bile rise in Adrian's throat. Randall's warning about an infection returned.

Running his tongue over his lengthening canines, Adrian

unslung his rifle and unlocked the safety. The female ahead was in danger. *My female*, his cat rumbled. Adrian couldn't deny the instinct. He picked up his pace to a run...

Get UNTAMED INSTINCT now!

ALSO BY TAMSIN LEY

Galactic Pirate Brides series

Galactic Pirate Brides Box Set (Includes first 3 books)

Rescued by Qaiyaan

Ransomed by Kashatok

Claimed by Noatak

Mates for Monsters

Mer-Lovers Illustrated Collector's Edition (Includes first 3 books plus exclusive illustrations)

The Merman's Kiss

The Merman's Quest

A Mermaid's Heart

The Centaur's Bride

The Djinn's Desire

Khargals of Duras

Sticks and Stones

Alaska Alphas

Alpha Origins

Untamed Instinct

Bewitched Shifter

Midnight Heat

POST-APOCALYPTIC SCIENCE FICTION WRITTEN AS TAM LINSEY

Botanicaust

The Reaping Room

Doomseeds

Amarantox

ABOUT THE AUTHOR

Once upon a time I thought I wanted to be a biomedical engineer, but experimenting on lab rats doesn't always lead to happy endings. Now I blend my nerdy infatuation of science with character-driven romance and guaranteed happily-ever-afters. My monsters always find their mates, with feisty heroines, tortured heroes, and all the steamy trouble they can handle. I promise my stories will never leave you hanging (although you may still crave more!)

When I'm not writing, I'll be in the garden or the kitchen, exploring Alaska with my husband, or preparing for the zombie apocalypse. I also love wine and hard apple cider, am mediocre at crochet, and have the cutest 12-pound bunny named Abigail.

Interested in more about me? Join my VIP Club and get free books, notices, and other cool stuff!

www.tamsinley.com

ACKNOWLEDGMENTS

To all my readers out there who email me, message me on Facebook, like and share my posts, and leave reviews on my books, I couldn't keep writing without you. You mean the world to me. Thank you!

Made in the USA
Las Vegas, NV
31 May 2021